LOVE UNLOCKED

Appreciation for the author

"A relatable story with a strong message about the importance of family – both entertaining and enlightening!"

– Shabana Azmi

(Veteran actress and Padma Bhushan awardee)

"The book shows how love has the power to impact individuals and create a positive change."

– Raell Padamsee

(CEO and Managing Director of ACE Productions and Numero Uno Productions)

"Love Unlocked is an interesting book which probes deep into relationships. The strains are captured brilliantly and portray the healing power of love."

– Surojit Gupta,

(Associate Editor, *The Times of India*)

"A fluid story about complicated human emotions told in the most relatable manner. You start picturising every chapter like it is a scene from a film playing before you. The author skilfully plays the trick of making you initially relate to the protagonist and also stand apart from her. An enjoyable, must-read book for those who feel deeply for family ties."

– Priti J. Nair

(Founder Director, Curry –Nation Brand Conversations)

"Love Unlocked delivers a poignant social message without being overtly obtrusive. As a physician myself, I am also grateful to Ms Bhatnagar for setting the story in the backdrop of a very relatable healthcare crisis and acknowledging the selfless service of the medical fraternity. The novel underscores the importance of family harmony, especially during these challenging times. Medicines can cure, but love can heal. This is exactly the message that shines forth through this meticulously crafted novel."

– Dr A. Raghuvanshi

(MD & CEO, Fortis Healthcare)

LOVE UNLOCKED

Kavita Bhatnagar

Srishti
PUBLISHERS & DISTRIBUTORS

Srishti Publishers & Distributors
A unit of AJR Publishing LLP
212A, Peacock Lane
Shahpur Jat, New Delhi – 110 049
editorial@srishtipublishers.com

First published by
Srishti Publishers & Distributors in 2022

10 9 8 7 6 5 4 3 2 1

This is a work of fiction. The characters, places, organisations and events described in this book are either a work of the author's imagination or have been used fictitiously. Any resemblance to people, living or dead, places, events, communities or organisations is purely coincidental.

The author asserts the moral right to be identified as the author of this work.

For Devika and Sarthak.
Your unbridled love sustains me.

Acknowledgements

The author thanks with love –

Sanjiv Sarin for planting the seeds of this one and helping with the narrative.

Dr Vishal Chhabra, not just for his therapeutic presence, but for his insightful inputs.

Nidhi Sharma, Neha Bhatnagar and Sheel Ratan Bhatnagar for the initial feedback and suggestions. Coffee is surely due!

Shobhit Arya for resolving so many dilemmas and being my go-to friend.

Bharat Gade for his magical wand.

Arup Bose, Stuti, Vini Bhati and the whole team of Srishti Publishers for the faith and collaboration in this journey.

And finally, my rock – my entire family for their circle of blessings and affection.

"I wish it need not have happened in my time," said Frodo.

"So do I," said Gandalf, "and so do all who live to see such times. But that is not for them to decide. All we have to decide is what to do with the time that is given us."

– J.R.R. Tolkien

Prologue

As Priyanka carefully applied the anti-wrinkle cream around her eyes, she looked at herself in the mirror. There were no wrinkles anywhere yet. She had just turned forty and was very conscious about maintaining her youth. Even though she had retained her petite figure of early twenties, with age, she had become a little more rounded now. She preferred to wear her long, dark brown hair either in a plait or a bun. And her eyes were normally hidden behind big spectacles. Inspite of having a pleasing appearance, she did not consider herself to be pretty.

As she looked at herself in the mirror, she thought to herself for the umpteenth time.

Why did Varun marry me? He is so handsome and good-looking!

She then smiled to herself as she recalled her courtship days. Varun broke her out of her musings as he hugged her from behind.

"Oops, I was startled!" Priyanka said.

"Who else it will be, sweetheart?" Varun said, nuzzling her. "Unless you have something naughty going on in your life which I don't know about."

Varun Chopra was an attractive man, with a fair complexion, wavy black hair and sharp features. Tall and well built, he looked much younger, even though he was forty-two years old. He was inching towards the vice president's post in a reputed pharmaceutical company. His professional success further added a warm glow to his striking face. He loved his family dearly and was in a content place, both personally and professionally.

"I tell you, you don't need these creams. You are fine, just the way you are," he said, still holding Priyanka close. She hugged him back and then, continued to finish her daily ritual of applying the night cream.

Priyanka had always been very particular about maintaining her external beauty. Possessing a deep knowledge of the cosmetics to be used for daily beauty regime, she applied various kinds of creams to sustain her facial glow. The only difference being that now, she had advanced to anti–wrinkle creams from simple moisturizers. In terms of her professional journey, she had also progressed to being the HR head in a software firm. Varun's company had provided them with a well-furnished, sea facing apartment in Bandra.

It was 2032 and both Varun and Priyanka had come a long way, not just in their careers but in life. Priyanka loved her life. She was always grateful to god for all her blessings.

Varun settled down to finish a presentation. After Priyanka completed her routine, she called out to her children Shrey, who was eleven years old and Abhiraj, who was eight years old. They were playing with their grandparents in the bedroom.

As they heard their mother's voice, they came running towards her. They were full of life, the two joy balls as Priyanka fondly called them. Bright and naughty kids, they loved to cuddle up to their parents at bedtime daily. They often demanded for a story, but tonight, they seemed to be in a talkative mood.

"Mumma, you know Archie in my class. She was very sad today," said Shrey, while Abhiraj fiddled with the TV.

"And why was that? Did you ask her?" Priyanka asked absent-mindedly as she was preoccupied with thoughts of the menu for tomorrow's meals.

"Yes, but she was not talking to anyone. I am her best friend so I gave her a chocolate, and then she told me."

"What did she share?" Priyanka got curious. Shrey's words brought her to the present immediately.

"Mumma, she is so unhappy. Her father and mother fight a lot. Yesterday also, they had a big quarrel. Archie was scared. She hid in the bathroom and cried there. Her mother did not even try to find her. She just went to sleep without any dinner. That is not good," Shrey narrated innocently.

Priyanka nodded. Then, she said in a thoughtful tone.

"I hope you were able to cheer her up. Don't leave her alone in school. Check that she eats her tiffin too."

"Yes, mumma. She also asked me if my parents also fight. But I said that they don't. You and daddy never fight," Shrey said happily in his sing-song voice.

Priyanka was startled by this observation. Varun also looked up from his work and their eyes met. Both of them smiled, as if feeling proud of their strong bond. They had gone through a lot together and their relationship had strengthened because of a variety of experiences.

"Enough of the chatter, kids! Go and brush your teeth!"

Both the kids obeyed their mother and rushed to the bathroom.

She then, went to check on papaji and mummyji. Both her in-laws were very affectionate and cooperative. Priyanka valued their presence and thrived on their support. They were in their seventies now and needed care. There was a maid who took care of them in the day, but mostly both Varun and Priyanka attended to all their needs. They were already asleep when Priyanka peeped into their room. She felt the soft Mumbai breeze on her face as she closed all the windows before returning to her room. She finally lay in the bed, stroking Abhiraj's soft hair.

"Tell me a story," the younger one said.

"Yes," Shrey immediately echoed.

"Shall we start *Gulliver's Travels* today?" Priyanka referred to the classic novel she had just bought for them.

"No," Shrey pouted. "I want to hear that story which you told me last week."

"Which one?" Priyanka tried to recall.

"The one in which you, daddy, dadu and dadi are there. The story of the virus."

"Why do you want to listen to it again? Let's read something different," Priyanka said, trying to dissuade Shrey. She did not like revisiting that time again. But Shrey did not give up and was joined by Abhiraj.

"Come this side, both of you!" Varun spoke as he removed his glasses. He knew too well that Priyanka preferred not to go back in time. A past from where they had all emerged victorious in every sense.

"Mumma is tired. Today, I will tell you a new story!" The excited kids turned towards him and soon, they were lost in a fantasy world.

Galvanized by the demands of children, Priyanka's mind had already started racing back to the past. She wanted to avoid the painful memories, but they had been stirred up today. First by Shrey's candid statement that his parents did not fight and then, by the mention of the virus.

She tried to sleep, but instead, she saw her childhood. She saw Shikha, Sapna, ma and dad.

1

Borivali Days

Born in 1992, Priyanka Malhotra was the elder child of Sanjay and Mamta Malhotra. They were a middle-class family living in Mumbai.

Sanjay worked in an insurance company as a development officer. They lived in a small two-bedroom rented apartment in Borivali. Priyanka and Shikha were his two daughters. He was very fond of them. Mamta was a homemaker and a loving mother. The atmosphere in their home was liberal. Though their means were limited, they dreamed freely.

Sanjay always wanted his daughters to be happy. As they were growing up, he rarely put any restrictions on them. He wanted to make them strong and independent. And when

Mamta would sometimes worry about their settling down after marriage. Sanjay would laugh it off.

"Our daughters are smart, Mamta! They will be able to manage everything well!"

❖

As the girls grew up, they got used to having their own way. With a difference of three years between them, Priyanka would often try to bully Shikha and dominate her. Shikha would complain to their father, who would always side with Priyanka. Mamta would then step in to balance the situation.

Priyanka was very average in her studies. In fact, she had even flunked once in junior school. On the contrary, Shikha was the one who excelled academically.

As Priyanka entered her teens, she would often find herself feeling jealous of her younger sister as Shikha was better looking. She would still spend hours in front of the mirror, striking different poses to figure out which one looked best. She had a petite figure but her nondescript features made her look simple. She longed to be fair and alluring. Her wheatish complexion complemented her long, brown hair but she constantly compared it with Shikha's jet black mane. As she graduated to class tenth, she started using spectacles. This further added to her complex of not being beautiful. She focussed a lot on her clothes in order to look attractive. She had also realized that blue colour suited her best, so she had many clothes in that shade.

School had passed off in a daze. Apart from being conscious of her looks, she had few memories from that time. Just home to school and then back home! The commute itself took more than an hour each way. Priyanka would be tired by the time she got back home, with no energy to do anything more. Moreover, studies didn't interest her much.

As she entered her teenage years, she had a strong desire to have a boyfriend who would pamper her. She was studying in an all-girls school so there weren't many opportunities to meet boys. She, however, had a huge crush on Rahul, the cute boy who lived two blocks away. He considered her a friend, and as much as she tried, he wouldn't respond to her in any other way.

All the other boys in the neighbourhood appeared too filmi for Priyanka. Not that she didn't like films. They were the major source of entertainment while growing up. The whole family would go together on a weekend. It was always the morning show as the tickets were a little cheaper at that time. And one popcorn was supposed to be shared amongst everyone.

❖

When his younger brother and wife passed away in a car accident, Sanjay had no option but to bring his niece Sapna, who was two years younger than Shikha, to his home. Priyanka and Shikha did not welcome her as they had to share their room and belongings with her. Sapna was already traumatised and stayed in her shell most of the time. Mamta expected Priyanka and Shikha to be caring towards her, but both sisters did not show any empathy towards her.

Priyanka had entered college by this time. She joined the prestigious Wilson College for a course in economics. Sanjay was very proud of her daughter's accomplishment. "You must make the most of it," he told her. She also wanted to get a grip now on her studies. However, she was distracted by her environment where the boys were very smart and the teachers less strict. Priyanka wanted to take her father's advice seriously and, at the same time not deprive herself of the fun of college life.

2

Boyfriend Bug

Priyanka started liking her college. Home appeared messy and crowded. Besides, being the eldest, Ma always expected her to do the chores – clean the rooms, make the beds, do the dusting and what not. She would just order whatever came to her mind. She had also decided that Priyanka must learn to cook.

"What will you do when you get married?" she had asked. That's when Priyanka made up her mind that she didn't want to learn cooking. She started making excuses. The one that always worked was 'I have to study.' But she would soon get bored with her textbooks and start texting on her mobile. And when her mother would find out, she would get really annoyed.

"If you are not studying, let's make chapatis. Today we'll make sure every single one is round and fluffy," ma would call out.

"Look at the ceiling here. Spider webs everywhere. Get a broom to clean them."

And Priyanka would have no option but to get up grudgingly. Trying to stay longer in the washroom didn't work either. There was just one among five people. Someone or the other always wanted to use it urgently. Almost the moment you went in, there would be a knock on the door. "Hurry up, I have to go urgently." Or ma would be at the door, "What are you doing for so long? Come out, soon."

College was a relief–a liberating space where she could be herself. There was no one to say anything. No one seemed to care whether she attended classes or bunked to hang around in the canteen. Going out with friends became the new way of life for her. She became the proverbial rebellious teenager and started living in an imaginary world where she was free of all responsibilities. That's when the boyfriend bug bit her.

As she made new friends, she discovered that most of them were going out with someone. Single people like her were very rare. Most of the girls were going steady since school itself, so she was already pretty late.

The idea of having a boyfriend was so exhilarating that she soon became determined to have one. She would often imagine what he would be like and what they would do together. Daydreaming became her constant activity.

Gradually, she totally lost interest in studies. What she really looked forward to were the parties. Invariably, it was one of the richer classmates who would invite friends over to their huge house in the suburbs. It would usually be a Saturday, and a lot of people would be there. There would be alcohol, food, music and dancing, and the party would continue until the early hours of the morning.

But Priyanka's curfew was 11 p.m. Though there was nothing explicitly said, her parents did not say anything as long as she came home by that time. Sometimes, there would be contributory parties. That's when each person was supposed to pay for themselves. Since Priyanka never had the money for them; she would refrain from attending those kinds of parties by making some excuse every time to her friends.

❖

"Why don't you start taking tuition, didi? Take a junior class student so you won't have to make much effort. Just twice a week would be enough," Shikha said to Priyanka. They were chatting with each other when Shikha came up with this suggestion which Priyanka really liked.

"That's great! But what would I teach? Maths is out of the question, Shikha."

"Take Hindi or English. You don't have to do much. Just repeat what is there in the textbook. And make them do the questions at the end of each chapter. I think the parents pay to keep the kids busy and for the relief of not having to bother about them for one or two hours," Shikha said candidly.

"How do you know so much?" Priyanka asked, suddenly suspicious.

"Aww, didi! You ask too many questions. I have seen friends doing it. I think I will start taking maths tuitions soon. Seventh or eighth grade, nobody senior!"

Priyanka wanted to ask, *Which friends? Why do you need money?*

She smelled a boyfriend somewhere. But she stopped herself.

Let's do that tactfully, some other time! She thought, in case Shikha clams up now. In fact, dad expected her to help Sapna with her studies. She might turn the whole idea into a commercial proposition.

Ma and dad were very pleased when she told them she wanted to start giving tuition to earn some money. She was a little surprised at their favourable reaction, till she realized they were assuming she wanted to help with the household expenses. They never imagined that it was to pay for her weekend parties.

It was at one of these parties that she met Dev.

❖

Dev was a dark, slim boy, of an average built and perhaps, a few years older than her. He had a small stubble when they met for the first time, which made his face look strangely attractive. Priyanka had been talking animatedly with a classmate who was waiting for her boyfriend to arrive. Dev strolled over and said hello. Both the girls responded. Right then, her classmate spotted her boyfriend and went to meet him, leaving Priyanka and Dev alone. They chatted for a while. Dev was studying commerce, but he was in a different college. He was drinking beer.

"Drink?" he offered, holding out his drink.

"I don't know!" Priyanka was unsure. She had refrained from having alcohol earlier at parties for the fear of her parents finding out.

"Come on, try a beer," coaxed Dev, sensing she was a non-drinker. "Nothing will happen. Beer has almost no alcohol. Here, let me get you a fresh drink."

He brought a pint for her.

"First rule of partying," he said, educating her. "Always take a fresh drink from the bar. Never take a drink from anyone, not even your best friend. Cheers!"

"Thanks, cheers!" Priyanka took a sip tentatively. It was bitter. She forced herself to swallow, trying not to make a face.

"Bitter?"

"Umm yes," Priyanka said. She was feeling a bit shy.

"Take another sip. After some time, the taste will smoothen out."

Priyanka tried again. This time, it was better. The aftertaste was strangely pleasant. But after half a bottle, she gave up her drink.

"Can I leave this?" she asked tentatively. "I don't think I can have more."

"Of course! Drink only as much as you are comfortable with."

They sat around in silence for some time, listening to the loud music that was being played in the next room. Priyanka decided that she didn't want to dance. She wanted to sit peacefully and enjoy this new sensation.

Soon, it was time for Priyanka to leave. She would have to rush if she wanted to reach home by 11 p.m.

"I must go now," she said. "Nice meeting you."

"So soon? I thought Cinderella's time was after midnight."

"Not for me, unfortunately," Priyanka said and smiled.

"Okay, bye. See you around." Dev got up and walked over to the next room.

She found it strange that he didn't even offer to walk her till the door.

"He isn't interested in me," she muttered to herself.

❖

Priyanka met Dev several times at different parties. It was clear that neither of them had a 'steady' relationship. And neither of them seemed to be enamoured enough to want to take the relationship to the next level. But it was still nice not to be alone at the parties. My 'party friend' was how Priyanka thought of him. So whenever they saw each other, they would hang around together.

Priyanka slowly graduated to having a full pint, but nothing more. Dev would have several. Often, Priyanka tried to count a few times, but gave up.

Soon, Priyanka felt that even after trying so much, she did not really belong to the parties. She was still an outsider, though now she had Dev by her side and a pint in her hand.

Why don't I fit in? What is it that I lack?

She wondered and concluded that her standard jeans and t-shirt outfit made her look very desi. She needed to be more glamorously dressed, like the other girls. Now that she knew the problem, she needed a solid solution to fix it.

Shikha came to her rescue. Priyanka asked her where she could buy such dresses at affordable prices. Shikha not only told her the names of the places, but also accompanied her to Linking Road –the middle class fashionista's paradise.

Priyanka was amazed at the variety of replica designer dresses of high-end brands. The street was full of affordable bags, shoes and clothes. The prices were reasonable and one could bargain as well. The lively atmosphere made it a shopper's delight.

Priyanka soaked it all in and began hunting for what she had in her mind. She and Shikha pooled in their pocket money and bought a couple of outfits each. Shikha being taller and well-built meant that they could not share each other's clothes. They splurged and even bought a pair of jeans for Sapna. They ended their shopping spree with a sumptuous Chinese meal.

Later, Priyanka pranced around in her new black mini skirt and an electric blue top that was more revealing than her staid t-shirts. She left her freshly shampooed hair open and brushed it till it shone. She was sure that now, she would blend well in the Saturday party. Shikha immediately commented on her new look.

"Oh my god, didi! Who are you trying to impress now?"

"Why? Does it look nice?" Priyanka asked as her cheeks turned red.

"Of course! You'll kill your boyfriend today."

"Shh! Shut up. You talk too much," she said, gesturing her to be quiet, but she did feel sexy in that dress. Fortunately, ma and dad did not see her go out, otherwise they might have stopped her.

❖

It was a large two-storey bungalow with a huge lawn in the posh Juhu area where the party was being held. The host's parents were away, so they had the entire place to themselves.

Priyanka entered with a lot of excitement. The whole place appeared to be teeming with youngsters, but she didn't know many people, though there were quite a few from her college. Her classmate had invited her, but she was nowhere to be seen. Dev was there, and as always, they gravitated towards each other. He let out a low whistle when he saw her.

"Wow, Cinderella at the party! Can I be your prince charming?"

"Shut up," she said, obviously pleased by his reaction.

"Let's sit down. I'm already a couple of beers down, waiting for my princess," Dev said, trying to flatter her.

"Don't be silly. Get me a pint too, please."

They sat on the stairs in the corridor, drinking their beers and chatting. There were several couples around, but everyone was too engrossed in themselves to notice others. The crowd moved to the lawns outside. From where they were sitting, they could hear Akon's 'Smack that' and the sound of dancing.

Then, Dev did something different. He reached out and drew her close. Priyanka realized this was the first time he had done that and she spontaneously hugged him back. After a while, his hands seemed to be all over her. Priyanka decided she liked the sensation and snuggled closer. Soon, he was unbuttoning her shirt and pulling up her skirt. She stiffened a little, not knowing how to respond.

Just then, a drunken fellow came lumbering down the stairs and banged into them. The shock was so sudden that Priyanka almost jumped out of her skin. She drew herself up, quickly buttoned her shirt and smoothened her skirt. Suddenly her skirt appeared to be much shorter than she thought it was. No matter how much she pulled and stretched, it barely covered her thighs.

"Sorry!" said the fellow and continued on his inebriated journey.

Dev walked over to the bar, got himself another beer and they sat down together again. But the moment was lost, the spell was broken. It was like old times now – sitting next to each other, not even holding hands. They did not speak much. They just absorbed the music – now Coldplay's song 'Fix You', playing in the background.

The hours passed away quickly. Before she realised, it was already past midnight. She got up quickly and almost ran, fearful of what would happen at home. She quickly combed her hair in the auto, but she knew it would remain dishevelled. Her clothes were all crumpled. She definitely looked like a mess.

Will her parents stop her from going out after this?

❖

It was 1 a.m. when Priyanka got back home. Dad opened the door.

Can he smell the alcohol in my breath? She wondered. And my short skirt – he will surely throw a fit.

But, to her surprise, her dad didn't say anything. He didn't even give her a look. Just a 'good night'. That was it.

The next day, ma reprimanded her for going to late outings. Shikha kept asking her the details, but Priyanka didn't have much to share. She felt sad that Dev was the best she could attract, despite her endeavours to find a hot date. She vented her frustration at Sapna and scolded her unnecessarily for not finishing her homework.

❖

Time flew by. Between the tuition classes and the weekend parties, there was never time for anything more. There were many boys with whom Priyanka spent time at the parties, but nothing became serious. Sometimes there would be some kissing, but that was all. She was just a 'party friend' to them, nothing more. She knew she was not good-looking enough to become their regular date. So, she consoled herself that at least, she had company during the parties. Finally, she was seeing a different world and enjoying as much as she could.

After a few weeks, she suddenly didn't see Dev at any of the parties anymore. He seemed to have simply disappeared. She wondered about him sometimes, but she didn't know anyone from whom she could find out. He was a loner. And strangely, they hadn't exchanged their mobile numbers. Priyanka knew that he wasn't husband material, so she would never be comfortable introducing him to her parents or even to her sister. Perhaps Dev thought the same about her too, she concluded wryly.

❖

Anand Sharma, the fresh entrant in college, was everything a girl would want in a boyfriend. He was tall with a six-pack body and an attractive face. His charming looks and amicable demeanour soon became the talk of the town. Girls vied with each other to get his attention and those in his class felt privileged to share space with him.

Priyanka was a year junior to him but they were together in the economics department. She was also swayed by his charming looks and personality. She wanted him to befriend her. But Priyanka knew that he would not even notice her in front of her college beauties. Yet strangely, she began to be possessed by a strong desire to 'win' him. This would not only make her popular in college but also fulfil her desire to have a real boyfriend. She knew she had to be smart. Instead of trying to seek his attention directly, she had a novel plan in mind. She had heard that Anand enjoyed extra-curricular activities like quizzes and actively participated in them. So, she started engaging with them as well.

The first step to be noticed by him was to beat his team in the intra college competition. She was preparing well but felt uncertain about winning. Her mind became active as she found out who was organising the event. Her face lit up as she realised it was a girl called Deepti from her class. She had caught Deepti making out with a boy behind the library in college. At that point, she had let it pass. But now, she knew how to leverage it. She made good use of the incident and soon, had the quiz questions with her.

Anand was confident of winning the quiz. After all, it was in his favourite subject of economics. He told his team mate and friend Kamal to relax as he sized up the opposing team. He perceived Priyanka and her team as a lousy opponent, someone who were incapable of defeating him. But to his chagrin, the lousy opponent answered each and every question correctly and won the quiz by a fair margin. He was startled by their performance. After the competition, he just went to congratulate the winners.

"Congratulations! You performed so brilliantly," Anand said as he shook hands with Priyanka.

Priyanka felt a thrill going down her spine at Anand's first touch. She smiled demurely at him and uttered, "Thanks!"

As Anand moved ahead, Priyanka realised she was losing out on her chance. She almost ran after him and asked, "Can you lend me some notes on cost benefit analysis? I'm finding it tough to understand and you know how absent-minded Professor Tyagi is. He just won't help."

The unsuspecting Anand nodded and agreed to get her the notes the next day. Priyanka spent the rest of the day smiling at her 'victory'.

❖

The next day, Priyanka dressed in a smart yellow top with tight jeans. She deliberately left her hair open to enhance her appearance. Shikha told her to opt for contact lenses. She was also starting her college. Bolder and smarter than Priyanka, Shikha often gave tips in fashion to Priyanka.

Priyanka's mind was filled with innovative ideas to charm Anand. Once in college, she positioned herself at the canteen which was near Anand's class so that he would not fail to see her when he stepped out. It happened precisely the way she had planned. Anand saw her and brought the notes over.

"Coffee?" she asked innocently and Anand couldn't say no. "I must say I was impressed by the way you won that quiz," Anand said, sizing her up. Priyanka blushed at the memory but then, made efforts to look nonchalant.

"I love such events. In fact, I would want to be part of the intercollege festival 'Rainbow', that is coming up soon. Our college is hosting the quiz competition and wouldn't it be lovely if we win it together?" she concluded, sipping her coffee but looking at Anand from the corner of her eyes.

Oblivious to the many stares they were getting, Anand pondered at the idea. "Yes, that would be a memorable win," he said. "I also want to hold that trophy in my hands. Let's do it – you, me and my friend Kamal – that would be the team for the Eco quiz," he concluded.

Priyanka almost sighed with relief. She had got what she wanted. Now she would have ample opportunities to spend time with him and make him fall for her, though she wasn't sure how.

❖

As the festival was less than a month away, Priyanka and Anand sprung into preparations. Kamal was preparing for the UPSC exam and his coaching classes kept him busy and away from college most of the time. Priyanka and Anand started to stay back in the library after college. They divided the topics and made notes. They would chat for long after they finished their work. Anand shared how he wanted to try for competitive exams in the banking sector after finishing his masters. He came across as a down-to-earth and unassuming person that only added to his appeal. However, Anand showed no signs of any intimacy towards Priyanka. Rather, he started treating her as a good friend. This was not what Priyanka had wanted; it was the second time it was happening to her. She again put her fertile mind to use in a bid to ensnare Anand.

One afternoon, after studying hard, Priyanka boldly asked Anand to catch a movie with her. Anand politely declined, saying he had to meet another friend and Priyanka was left smarting. Anand sensed her annoyance and after a few days, he himself offered to go to a movie with her. Priyanka was ecstatic. She also got a glimpse of Anand's appeasing nature that made her like him even more. She quickly started formulating her next steps.

As they entered the dark cinema hall, Priyanka squealed as she twisted her foot on the stairs. Anand held her to prevent her from falling and Priyanka gladly clung to him. Due to the darkness, he could not see her smile broadly. Priyanka continued to hold Anand's hand during the movie and felt satisfied when he did not try to disengage. They enjoyed the antics of Ant-Man and the movie was over too soon. Anand was still concerned about her foot and saw her off in an auto before going his way. Priyanka was very happy with the developments, so what if it meant a sprain in the ankle!

❖

"Didi, what's cooking? Despite your discomfort, I often see you smiling," Shikha commented one evening.

"Come on, spill the beans," she persisted. Priyanka told her about Anand and how they were coming close. Shikha found it hard to believe but didn't dispel her sister's dreamy notions. Unlike her, she was determined to be successful in her career first rather than getting involved in the boyfriend business.

Priyanka hobbled around in college for a few days, holding on to Anand for support whenever she could. She hoped this would brand them as a couple and then, Anand would actually be drawn towards her. But Anand seemed to be engrossed only in winning the quiz and kept studying hard for it.

A few days before the festival, Priyanka offered lunch from her tiffin to Anand. She could barely cook but passed on ma's cooking skills as hers. She was happy to see that the sumptuous meal impacted Anand. He asked her to bring food for him daily and said it was even better than his mother's cooking. Priyanka wished she had thought of this earlier but she lost no time in bringing new dishes for him every day and feeding him with bliss. However, Anand was still not responding to her as a boyfriend would and Priyanka decided she would have to do something drastic now.

❖

The weeklong festival soon started. The quiz competition was on the second day. The trio of Anand, Priyanka and Kamal did exceedingly well right from the start. They answered most of the questions correctly. Soon, the other teams were trailing and it was clear who would be the winner.

To their utter delight, they won the quiz and were awarded a huge trophy for the same. All three of them were ecstatic but Anand more so. Priyanka was quick to seize the moment.

"Hey, let's celebrate! Let's go to the rock show concert in the finale on Saturday. It will be the college band vs the IIT Mumbai band. It will be great fun." Anand agreed immediately as he was fond of music. Besides that, a lot of hype was being built for the finale.

As quiz winners, they got a complimentary invite to the concert. Kamal, as usual backed out, which is what Priyanka had anticipated. She spent the next two days deciding about her 'look'. She went to Linking Road to search for a new dress. Finally, she found just what she had in mind – a navy blue, knee length dress with a plunging neckline. She also bought matching footwear and accessories. She searched on YouTube about how she could style her hair and settled on a trending style with hair swept on one side, which she could do herself. Shikha teased her about her preparations but this time, Priyanka didn't confide in her. It was her big secret. Dad was happy that she had won the quiz and didn't object to her going for the concert.

Priyanka got ready on Saturday with some trepidation. While she wanted her plan to work, she was not sure of what would happen if it misfired. She shrugged those thoughts and focused on looking good enough for Anand. As Shikha and Sapna complimented her, she knew she had succeeded in her efforts to transform into a diva from the plain-looking girl Jane Eyre, well almost! She covered her dress with a dull coloured shrug so that ma won't object to it and stepped out for her big date.

Anand looked dapper as ever in a navy-blue striped T-shirt and jeans. He greeted Priyanka warmly, "Oh my god! You look different. I couldn't recognise you for a moment," he exclaimed.

"Come, let's go," he took her by the hand and led her towards the front rows to catch the concert.

The atmosphere was electric and as the evergreen numbers by bands like AC-DC, Def Leppard and Pink Floyd were played out. Both of them swayed to the lively beats. The atmosphere became even more charged as the more popular numbers by Linkin Park and Green Day enthused the energetic crowd.

After a while Priyanka, mindful of her deadline, whispered in Anand's ears to get some beer. Anand nodded and so they left the concert and went towards the hostel. Priyanka's friend Aman was there, waiting for them. Priyanka explained to Anand how she had asked Aman to do them this favour. Aman not only got them beer, but also offered them to feel comfortable in his hostel room rather than move around outside. So after Aman left, they settled down in the small room and said cheers heartily. Priyanka enjoyed drinking beer and she presumed that Anand was glad to give her company. As they came to the second pint, she leaned closer to Anand. He looked questioningly at her. In response she cosied up to him further.

Anand pushed her away and said sternly, "Look, I think of you as a friend and all this has never crossed my mind. Let's not spoil our friendship." Priyanka was stunned. She had not expected this admonishment. She mumbled a sorry and said she wanted to leave.

In silence, Anand dropped her till the station. On her way back, Priyanka grappled with multiple feelings and thoughts. Not only did her plan backfire, but she also made a fool of herself. She just hoped that Anand wouldn't make her a laughingstock in college now.

Oh, why had I even thought that I could lure a person like Anand? She thought to herself. Shikha let her in and was dismayed to see her crestfallen face.

"What's wrong? Didi, please share with me, you will feel lighter," she said gently. Priyanka almost cried on hearing the caring words and slowly poured her heart out to Shikha. "I feel like such a fool," she concluded. Shikha sighed and in a moment of role reversal, stroked her elder sister's hair. "Just avoid him now, didi," Shikha gave sound advice. "You will soon forget about it. And also now it's your last semester. Please try and focus on your career prospects. Dad expects you to be financially independent soon." As Sapna started to wake up upon hearing their conversation, they deliberately avoided her and slept.

The next day was thankfully a Sunday and she didn't have to go to college. She was dreading the thought of facing Anand. She decided to skip college for a few days. Perhaps he would let go of the incident by then.

She resumed college after three days and remained confined to her classes and her girl gang. Aman tried to tease her about Saturday night but seeing her sour looks, he quickly shut up. Thankfully, she did not meet Anand personally and gradually started to think less about the incident by then.

Her attempt to make a boyfriend thwarted. Priyanka started to focus again on her career prospects as the academic year ended. She decided to pursue a job in office administration after her graduation.

3

Arranged Marriage

Sanjay returned home one evening in a jolly mood. He asked Mamta to make tea and then asked Priyanka to join him.

"Beta, how are things with you? You keep so busy that we hardly talk nowadays."

Priyanka rattled off about her tough curriculum and how she was trying to do well in her upcoming exams.

"Dad, I get very tired by the time classes finish and then, I stay back to make notes. My teachers are expecting our batch to really perform well. The journey back home also takes so long. When I come back, I just want to lie down and sleep," she replied.

Sipping tea, Sanjay revealed that he had a marriage proposal for Priyanka. Ma was exhilarated but Priyanka was not so excited. Thoughts of Anand came back to her. She wished that she had a boyfriend whom she could have introduced to her father.

"Dad," she said, "I don't think I want marriage just now. Let me do a course in business administration and then, get a job." She wanted to delay the matter.

"This is too good a proposal to refuse. My friend in office has suggested his uncle's son for you. The Chopras are a well settled family, in Mumbai itself. Their son, Varun is a medical representative. He is their only child.

"See, Priyanka, you know I don't force you for anything and marriage is a big decision, no doubt. But I feel, you should consider it and also understand our situation. I have two more girls to settle after you. My retirement is approaching and I would want to be free of all my responsibilities at the earliest. Sapna is still young but Shikha would soon be of marriageable age. I hope you understand my perspective," he concluded.

Ma backed the idea and said, "At least we can fix a meeting and see how it goes. Priyanka, you know we will not force you but there's no harm in meeting them. Then you can decide."

Hearing all this, Priyanka agreed reluctantly. No harm in meeting the boy!

Sanjay immediately asked his friend to fix a meeting with the boy and his family. The meeting was fixed on Sunday. It was already Thursday and Mamta wanted to ensure that everything was impeccable. She told Shikha to help Priyanka with her appearance. Sapna was directed to help in the kitchen. Priyanka was not really inclined to dress up to impress, but having agreed to the meeting she knew she would have to do her part now. She was also overcoming the rejection meted out to her by Anand. However, she hoped that this Varun guy would turn out to be as good, if not better than Anand.

4

Finding Love

Priyanka looked in the mirror and smiled. She looked good in the bridal attire – a deep red zardozi lehenga with golden *odhni*. Her hard work in selecting the rich ensemble had paid off. She was dreamy-eyed – a pretty, young girl, about to enter the best phase of her life. Her slim figure was accentuated by the bright outfit and her long hair was held in a thick bun. No artificial braids for her. Flowers adorned her hair. And she had decided to wear contact lenses today as a special luxury. It made her look angelic. As the beautician finished her makeup, Priyanka's could not help but admiring herself.

How did I arrive at this beautiful moment? Her mind went back to the last few months.

❖

The meeting with Varun and his family had gone off better than she had imagined. Alka and Jagat, Varun's parents were typical middle class folks whose son was at the centre of their existence.

Varun was handsome and charming. He had made Priyanka's heart skip a beat just at the first glance. She realised that she was actually getting a good match. She had appeared demure in a blue sari. Varun's father clarified right at the beginning that they had no demands except that the wedding should be done with all the proper rituals. This lifted a load off her father who had been scrounging and saving for the marriages of the three girls. Immediately, a sense of genuine camaraderie seemed to develop between the two families.

Ma hit off well with Varun's mother – they came from a similar background and upheld the same beliefs and value systems. When they chatted, they seemed to go on and on about general household issues – how difficult it was to get house help and how pure ghee, no longer, had the taste which it used to and how everything came with preservatives and chemicals.

Priyanka was surprised when she heard ma talk about her skills at house work. She couldn't believe her ears.

Was this the same ma who would find fault with everything she did? She couldn't even serve a glass of water properly, her ma would say. And now, even her chapati making skills were supposed to be superb!

Varun and Priyanka were given a chance to talk to each other alone. They decided to go out for a stroll to the nearby park.

Both were awkward and tongue tied. Priyanka was very nervous, though she was trying to pretend that everything was normal. Then, she realized that Varun was trying his best to remain calm and composed too. That made her feel better! She felt her confidence coming back.

How should I break the ice? Should I ask something simple? Anything simple like, did they have trouble finding the house? To get Varun to start talking. Then she stopped herself. He'll think I am too forward, she thought.

Finally, Varun spoke. "What are your hobbies?" He almost blurted out the question.

What a question to ask? Priyanka thought. Hadn't he read the long biodata they had sent? Priyanka knew Varun's by heart. Including the spelling errors!

He could have at least used a spell check!

She decided to continue being the shy, timid girl. That's what was expected of her. He seemed to be a decent sort. It was worth trying to get him to say 'yes'.

"I like to watch movies. It's fun. It's our regular family outing," Priyanka said. Varun responded that his parents were not very fond of movies but he went out once in a while with friends.

"And I can cook a little also," continued Priyanka. "But not as well as ma was saying. She always praises whatever I make."

That wasn't true, but did it really matter? She thought. Varun would never find out what ma actually said. Ma would find fault with everything she did. And she couldn't make chapatis, to save her life. She could never get the dough right. It would either be too hard or too soft.

And round chapatis? It was as if round as a shape did not exist. But as of now, it was important to impress Varun.

She also talked about how she wanted to find a job and be financially independent.

Varun heard her out and kept quiet.

"What about you?" Priyanka asked finally.

Then Varun started talking. He told her about his job and how he had joined the company soon after college. He was expecting a raise soon.

"I am very close to my parents. They have brought me up with love and now it's my turn to take care of them. Papa will be retiring soon and I hope to give them a good quality life after that."

Priyanka, who was rather smitten by his looks, was barely listening to him. She was not really assessing him but dreaming about what life would be if she was married to Varun. She was happy there was a chance of getting a good-looking husband and a decent family, in Mumbai itself. She could still be near her parents after marriage. Varun's family was much better off than hers and Varun looked like the type who would have a great career – sincere, hardworking, and intelligent. She would have a handsome husband and a more luxurious life. Finally, she would be the pampered one. No more counting where every rupee was being spent.

The immediate problem was, how to make Varun say "yes". She wondered what to do. She couldn't hold his hand or give him a hug. Shy and demure was all she was supposed to be! She agreed with him in whatever he said to boost his ego.

When they came back from the walk, all eyes were on Varun, trying to fathom his thoughts. Varun just looked at his mother and gave an imperceptible nod. Priyanka, who was watching him closely from the corner of her eyes, saw it immediately. Her parents seemed to have missed it. But was that a yes or a no? Priyanka couldn't decide.

Finally, Varun's father thanked everyone and prepared to leave. He said that they would give their reply in a week or so. They had to consult within the family first. Those days were the longest in Priyanka's life. What made it worse was that she had to pretend that everything was normal. She couldn't show her keenness about the proposal. She couldn't ask her parents anything. She just went about her work listlessly.

Soon after ten days, dad received a call from Varun's father. The relief and happiness on his face said it all. The answer was a clear yes. Priyanka was over the moon. She had to pretend to be calm, but she was certain that her loud heartbeats would give away her excitement.

Right after that blissful moment, she began daydreaming about her comfortable future. She imagined herself to be eating ice-cream and watching TV, lying comfortably in bed. She could never do that with ma. And in the evenings, She would dress up and go out with Varun for dinner. All thoughts of a successful career flew out of the window as she dreamed about her new life.

❖

The sound of the band playing snapped her out of her thoughts and made her realize that the *baaraat* had arrived. Shikha and Sapna left her side to peep out and have a look at the groom and his friends. Ma and dad were already busy in welcoming them. Priyanka was exhilarated at how the magic of destiny took her to where she belonged. The cheerful ambience took her back to the exciting days of their marriage preparation.

❖

Dad had asked for six months' time to make the marriage arrangements. Priyanka knew he needed time to arrange the money. She and Shikha both had saved a little from their tuition. A marriage was an expensive affair, so they wanted to do their bit. Their father was reluctant to take it. But Priyanka insisted.

"Dad, you have to take this money. It is not much. Just around two lakhs but I am sure it will help a little."

"Where did you get so much money from?" Ma interjected.

"I have learned from you to save, Ma. And a friend advised us, so we invested in a mutual fund which gave good returns," Shikha spoke.

"Our daughters have grown up," commented dad, his voice filled with immense pride. "But beta, it is your money. You have earned it."

"So the money you earn is your money? We shouldn't be spending it? No, dad. This is family money."

Saying that, Priyanka went to her room and came back with a cheque.

"Please use it however you want." She put the cheque in her father's hands.

Sapna was watching all this in her quiet manner. Suddenly she spoke, "Tauji, I want to contribute too. I may not be earning but please feel free to use my mother's jewellery for didi."

With tears in her eyes, Mamta hugged her. She was very proud of her daughters.

❖

A December marriage suited everyone. There were no school exams so relatives with children would be able to join. And you could dress up better during winters. The women had to brave the cold, but they seemed to prefer it. The intervening months would also enable her to go out with Varun – something she longed for. She wanted to show him off to her friends. With these thoughts, she was glad that the marriage date was fixed for 2 December.

Varun asked her out on a date the very next week itself. She thought he was a little bold to call her directly and ask her out. She agreed, right away. It was only when she went to ma to inform her that she came to know that Varun had followed the traditional protocol. First, his mother had called up Priyanka's mother to seek her concurrence. Then, Varun called dad and requested his permission to ask Priyanka to go out with him.

Priyanka didn't know whether she should be happy at Varun's proper behaviour or disappointed that he wasn't as bold as she had imagined him to be.

Though Saturday was just two days away, it seemed as if time had stood still. Priyanka fretted about what to wear.

Should I wear jeans? Or a salwar-kameez? Not a sari definitely – it would be too formal. Colour? I had worn blue when Varun had come home. Should I wear a brighter colour this time? Maybe yellow? No, that would be too bright.

She decided to ask her mother. Her mother was in the kitchen, doing her unending chores.

"Ma, what should I wear on Saturday?" she asked.

"Why don't you wear that nice blue suit mamaji gave you?"

"But I wore blue last time also."

"Yes, but it's a different shade. It looks nice on you."

But I don't want the suit to look nice – I want me to look nice. She thought to herself. But she remained quiet. No point getting into an argument.

"And keep your hair open. You have nice hair. Boys like long, flowing hair." Her mother gave her additional advice.

In the normal course of events, she would have retorted by saying, "How do you know? How many boys have you gone out with?" But this was not the occasion.

"And beta, be careful. You know how boys are. Even though he is your future husband, stay within limits. He will respect you for that."

Just what I need right now! It was my fault! Why did I go to her for advice? Now the flood of advice will start. A quick exit would be best.

"Thanks, ma," she said before hurrying away. "I'll check if that suit is ironed."

She went back to her room and lay down on the bed, daydreaming.

Where will I go on Saturday? An expensive restaurant? Or just walk down a beach or sit in a park somewhere? What will we do?

Ma's advice got her thinking. They have to hold hands and kiss at least, she decided.

But would Varun want to do anything more? Should I let him? If he doesn't take the initiative, should I encourage him a little?

❖

The first date was memorable just because it was so boring. Nothing happened!

Varun was stiff and awkward. Perhaps, this was the first time he was going out with a girl. He was tongue-tied most of the time. His only conversation was about his work and future plans. Nothing romantic!

He had come exactly at six in the evening. Priyanka was ready to meet him in a peach, floral, knee length dress with her hair tied loosely. When he rang the bell, Shikha opened the door.

"Jijaji!" she announced loudly as she opened the door.

Why couldn't she stay away, with her pretty face and likeable mannerisms? Priyanka thought.

Ma and dad met him first.

"Be back in time," dad told him. 'Is 11:00 p.m. okay?"

"I was thinking more like 9:30 p.m. to 10 p.m. Thanks for the extra hour," Varun said.

What a strange reply. Priyanka thought. *Maybe he is like that only*.

Earlier, dad had given her four-thousand rupees. Priyanka knew that it was a lot of money for him.

"But dad, you know I have my pocket money also. I don't need that money," she had protested.

"Keep it! Share the bill," he said simply.

Priyanka's eyes were filled with tears. She didn't know what to say.

❖

Once they left home, they took cab and went to Juhu beach. Priyanka hadn't used a cab for ages. Bus and locals are what she survived on. Auto was a luxury. It was only used when she was getting very late that she preferred using a cab.

They walked up and down the beach. Then, they decided to sit down somewhere. Priyanka didn't want to spoil her dress and sit on the sand, like all the other people around. Finally they found a little rock jutting out which seemed a little less dirty.

He didn't appear to be a bad sort. After the initial awkwardness, he started talking. She found him to be a caring and supportive person. Varun talked about his aspirations, how he wanted to clear competitive examinations and be a government officer, just like his father. He told her how, in the final year of his college, he had given his resume to the placement cell, just for experience's sake. However, he was selected by this big pharmaceutical MNC that offered him a very good package. His father had opposed his decision to accept a private sector job initially, but seeing Varun's enthusiasm he agreed. Thus, Varun joined K&G Pharmaceutical immediately after his graduation and there had been no looking back ever since. In fact, he was going to be promoted very soon.

Priyanka felt happy with whatever she heard. For her, Varun's present salary itself would be a lot. If Varun aspired to earn more, that would take her closer to her ideal life. She would live in the lap of luxury. Maybe they would buy a car also. Buying a car was a big thing for her. While travelling in buses and local trains, she would look wistfully at the cars passing by. Especially during the monsoons! Commuting in Mumbai was not pleasant during the rains.

Priyanka stole a look towards Varun. He was still talking animatedly about his job and his boss. Her thoughts strayed a little.

What kind of a boy was he? He hadn't even touched me yet. All the boys I had known would have had their arms around her within the first ten minutes.

"This won't do," she decided. "Time to take charge," she told herself.

She looked around. The sun had set a long time ago. "It's getting dark. Let's move to a lighted area," she told Varun.

Varun got up immediately. "Sorry. I should have realized that. Let's go," he said, flustered.

Priyanka held out her hand for help in getting up. Varun reached out and held her hand. An electric shock seemed to go through him as he touched her. Probably, this was the first time he was touching a girl like this.

They moved towards the pav-bhaji stalls nearby. There were people everywhere. It seemed that no one in Mumbai ate at home during weekends.

As they walked on the sand, Priyanka stumbled. Varun reached out instinctively and held her. "Careful," he said. "Are you okay?"

"I think so," replied Priyanka. "I may have pulled a muscle. Let's see."

She started walking with a slight limp. Varun had continued to hold her hand which brought her a lot of satisfaction.

"Hungry?" Varun asked as they neared a stall. "Want to have a pav-bhaji?"

Priyanka saw her dream of a fancy restaurant vanish.

Pav-bhaji? She thought to herself. *Who has pav-bhaji on their first date?*

Varun noticed her hesitation.

"We can go somewhere else, if you want," he offered.

"No, why waste money? Pav-bhaji is good. But I can't have a full plate. Want to share?" she quickly covered up.

Varun nodded in satisfaction. Her approach to money was right.

"Sure," he said aloud. "Let's share a plate."

Just wait, Varun Chopra! *I'll show you how to spend money soon.* Priyanka thought.

The cab ride back was uneventful. Varun had continued to hold her hand. But that was all. He didn't try to venture further and Priyanka was not in the mood either.

When they reached home, Varun said goodbye at the door itself. He didn't want to come in. He said that he would continue with the same cab and didn't want to keep it waiting.

Ma and dad were sitting at the dining table, talking.

"How was it?" ma asked with a smile. "Everything went well?"

"Yes, ma," Priyanka replied simply. "All fine. I am tired. I'll go and change. Good night."

She suddenly remembered the money dad had given her. She hadn't spent it. For a moment she thought of returning it, but then changed her mind as her dad told her to keep it.

Shikha was waiting for her in the bedroom, wide awake. She started talking in whispers so as not to awaken Sapna.

"How was it, didi? How was jijaji?" she asked excitedly.

"Very boring," replied Priyanka. "We had pav-bhaji and came back."

"What all happened? What all did you do? Did he kiss you? Tell me," Shikha pleaded.

"Nothing happened. No kiss. Not even a hug. We just held hands."

"Aww, how unromantic! This won't do, didi. You have to do something next time. Boys need to be taught these things."

"Don't worry about me. You worry about yourself," chided Priyanka, effectively ending the conversation.

❖

The six months before marriage passed off in a daze. There was a lot to do. Every day, when she came back from college, ma was ready with a long list of shopping to be done. Sometimes ma would come towards college in the afternoon and they would leave together for shopping expeditions. And at home there were endless things to do. Wedding cards, guest lists, transport and staying arrangements of the outstation relatives, catering arrangements, menu – there was no end to the preparations.

The bridal dress took the longest to decide. After endless discussions with ma and Shikha, they selected the traditional lehenga with a modern touch. Priyanka wanted it to be heavily embroidered so that it gave a rich look. The rest of the ladies were to wear saris so hunting for them took them to many shops in different localities. They ended up overspending and Mamta grew anxious. There was a separate shopping list for gifts for the groom's family. Mamta made sure at least that was within their budget.

And amid all this, Varun grew extremely restless about meeting her frequently. He suddenly seemed to have all the time in the world for her.

Didn't he have any work to do in the office? She should visit his office someday and see if he actually worked there. How did he have so much free time? She thought.

He would call at all times and wanted to talk for hours on the phone. She could not spare so much time in the day and at night, sleep would overtake her. He wanted to meet her almost every day. He seemed to be free for her all the time. But deep down, Priyanka enjoyed all the attention from her family and Varun. She kept visualizing her happy and romantic married life. At times, she bunked her classes in the afternoon to spend time with him.

Varun picking her up and dropping her back in the middle of the day meant that she could show him off to everyone in college. Her intentions of studying further and finding a job had vanished in thin air. She was egged on by her friends who told her to take life easy and simply enjoy with her good-looking husband.

The first time Varun came to pick her up, all her friends rushed to the college gate to have a look at him. Varun felt conscious as he realized that he was the cynosure of all eyes but he had eyes only for Priyanka. She had spent hours agonizing what to wear that day. She really wanted to look attractive. But she couldn't be overdressed for college either.

Ma had been no help. She just said, "Wear anything. You look good in whatever you usually wear."

But she knew about herself. She had to work really hard just to appear presentable. Not like Shikha!

Shikha looked good even in a shapeless nightgown, with hair all tousled. Finally she decided to wear her regular jeans and a top. The comfort level would give her some confidence.

They had gone to a park nearby. They walked up and down in the park for a while, then sat down on a bench. Priyanka felt a little awkward sitting there, doing nothing. But when she looked around, she saw a dozen of couples like them. No one even gave them a second look.

Soon this park became their twice-a-week routine. Even the bench they would sit on became fixed. Varun got into the habit of lying down, head on her lap, just like what most of the other couples seemed to be doing. The first time she hesitantly stroked his head a little. When she saw how much Varun was enjoying it, she got more comfortable and continued. Once she thought she would reverse the roles and lie down instead. But that became troublesome. Soon Varun's hands started straying. From stroking her head, they went down to her cheeks and then her neck. Though she was pretending to be asleep, with her eyes closed, her heart was beating so loudly that she thought Varun would hear it. Soon his hands would be lower down. But Varun appeared oblivious to everything. As if he was moving his hands absent-mindedly. Priyanka was confused.

Should she let him continue? After all, they were getting married. It wasn't as if this was the first time a boy had been touching her like that. And she wasn't even engaged to be married to those boys. Surely there could be no problem now? But what if Varun started thinking she was 'that' kind of girl? He was so conservative. Better to be safe!

She stirred and opened her eyes.

"Awake?" asked Varun.

"Umm yes. I think my back is hurting from this hard bench. Let's get up and take a walk."

"Okay," said Varun, trying to control the disappointment in his voice. He remained mostly silent for the rest of the time that day. To cover this awkwardness, Priyanka chattered brightly. He was still in a sour mood when they had said goodbye.

But Priyanka had learned her lesson. After that, she never lay on the bench again, tactfully blaming the hardness.

❖

Another time, Varun brought her a gift – a brown colour suit.

What an awful colour! She thought.

"How nice," she said, controlling her first reaction. "What is the occasion?" She smiled at him.

"No occasion. Just like that," said Varun, pleased with her smile.

"Thanks a lot. I really like it." Then, she looked at the label. "But it's the large size. I wear medium, sometimes small, depending on the style. Never mind. We'll go and exchange it."

"I bought it at a sale. They said no returns or exchanges. Sorry. I didn't check the size."

How cheap! The first gift you buy for your future wife is from a discount sale. Just wait till we are married. Then your true learning will start. Priyanka thought.

"Doesn't matter," she replied. "I'll get it altered. There is a tailor near our house who is very reasonable. I'll tell him to be careful. You see, when you alter a kurta, the design on the front can get spoiled."

"Sorry, I didn't know all these finer details," replied Varun simply.

If you'd gone to a decent shop instead of a roadside kiosk, they would have told you. She thought.

"It's really pretty. I'll save it for special occasions. Thanks a lot." She gave him a big smile and squeezed his hand.

Of course, the special occasion will never come.

❖

Priyanka remembered vividly when they kissed for the first time. As with holding hands, she knew she would have to initiate it. But she didn't know how to do that without appearing too forward.

In the end, it happened quite naturally. They had been going out for a couple of weeks by then. It was a warm, humid day. There was a mild breeze blowing, just enough to make sure you didn't sweat, but not enough to make the weather pleasant.

They were in the park and Varun was sitting at their usual bench. Priyanka was standing near him. She was about to make a comment on the weather, when Varun spoke, with excitement in his voice.

"I have some good news, today."

"What?" she asked, wondering if it was some message from his parents. Or maybe, the hall for the post-marriage reception had been booked.

"I am getting promoted. My boss called me today morning and gave me this news."

Priyanka was thrilled. More probably because she was expecting him to give some dull news. She bent down spontaneously and gave him a hug and a big kiss on both cheeks.

"Congratulations!" she exclaimed, still holding both his cheeks with her hands and planting one more kiss, this time on his lips.

Varun was overjoyed – more by her reaction than his actual promotion. He responded by pulling her closer and kissing her back. Priyanka sat down next to him and they held hands silently, happy just to be in each other's company.

The barrier broken, a welcome and goodbye kiss became a routine.

5

Honeymoon Over

Priyanka smiled to herself as she recalled all the memories. The buzz from the wedding guests got louder, almost drowning the songs the DJ was playing. Soon Shikha, Sapna and her friends led her to the stage.

As Varun smiled at her and their eyes met, Priyanka's mind went back again to the past, while she moved almost mechanically to perform the garland ceremony. Memories of all the events leading to her wedding came flooding back.

She recalled how Varun had asked her where she would like to go for their honeymoon and she had said that she had never been abroad. She wanted to, so she had even got her passport made, just in case she got a chance to go at a short notice. Varun had immediately applied for his own passport and that had built up the excitement within her. She enjoyed shopping for her wedding trousseau and gifts for Varun's family. She had been starry eyed for all these six months. She eagerly waited for the moment where she and Varun would become one in body and soul.

❖

A loud commotion interrupted her happy thoughts. She had put the garland on Varun and posed for the customary picture. It was Varun's turn to garland her, when one of his uncles appeared on the stage. He appeared a little tipsy. Priyanka wondered where he had got his drinks from. Alcohol was not being served. Both set of parents had been very clear on that.

Uncleji was almost shouting, definitely louder than what was necessary. "What kind of wedding is this? Nobody is taking care of the baaraatis. All are busy on stage. They have no time to welcome us and offer even a piece of sweet."

Dad rushed to placate him, as did papaji. They gently took him to one side of the hall, away from all the guests. At least fewer people will see the misbehaviour. He was calmed down with great difficulty. She saw papaji moving away, leaving dad to handle the situation.

Dad apologized profusely and gave him a box of sweets and a cash envelope. Varun watched all this without commenting on the situation. Priyanka was shocked.

How cheap! Why is my father bearing the brunt of his misbehaviour?

Her dream wedding had almost been spoiled. She wanted Varun or his father to tell that man to shut up but they had just kept quiet. And, her father had to do all the assuaging. Her mood was spoilt a little but she forced herself to smile.

Can't spoil the photographs! She thought. Varun tried a bit to cheer her up and she had to make a lot of effort to appear casual.

❖

As the wedding celebrations concluded, the *vidaai* ceremony began with sad songs in the background, Priyanka felt tears brimming in her eyes. Earlier, she had thought that she wouldn't cry. But now she had mixed feelings.

On one hand, she was leaving behind her father's home where she had always got what she wanted. On the other hand, she was going to a new life where love and luxury awaited her. As the dawn approached, Priyanka also entered her new home with hope and joy, the sordid incident of the wedding forgotten. She was keen to forge new bonds and lead a wholesome life. She could sense Varun echoeing her feelings as well. She believed that nothing could deter her from experiencing a beautiful life now. Tired from all the rituals and festivities, they both fell asleep soon after hitting the bed. The glass of milk kept on the bedside remained untouched.

On the next day itself, they left for their honeymoon. Priyanka's joy had known no bounds when Varun shared the destination. Hong Kong and Macau it was!

❖

The newlyweds started their week-long honeymoon with Macau. They flew to Hong Kong, holding hands and romancing all the way. The first stop being Macau, they took a ferry to Macau from Hong Kong airport itself. Both enjoyed the journey – a first for both of them and within two hours, they reached Macau – Asia's Las Vegas.

Varun had booked them into the famous Venetian for a day. He had saved for this trip and wanted to impress his lovely wife. And impressed she was!

The mesmerising sights of the grand Venetian swept her off her feet. She had never even imagined anything like it. Their suite was like a princess's room but the shopping arcade all around was too tempting to stay indoors. She changed into a new olive green dress and dragged Varun down to explore the hotel. Bright lights and cheerful sounds filled the entire area. The artificial sky on the dome made them lose track of time. The stores of all the big brands were present there, enticing them to spend endlessly. Varun knew they could not afford to shop there. He urged Priyanka to simply enjoy the captivating sights first. There was a canal flowing through parts of the hotel and there was a Venice style gondola ride available. Varun couldn't say no to that. It was a unique experience. Priyanka recalled and sang aloud,

Do lafzon ki hai, dil ki kahaani,
Kya hai mohabbat, kya hai jawaani.

It was the famous song featuring Amitabh Bachchan and Zeenat Aman from *The Great Gambler*.

Varun took lots of her pictures in different poses and Priyanka felt as if she was in heaven. She was even able to buy a scarf as a souvenir from one of the smaller shops.

❖

In the evening they walked around a bit and saw the heavenly musical fountain for a while. They were spellbound by the magical sights. They splurged on Chinese food and then, made their way to the casino inside the hotel. Both felt a little awkward as they were doing it for the first time. They moved around but could not dare to play any game. Just soaking in the atmosphere around provided them with high energy. They returned to their room after midnight and though tired, made love with passion. As Varun explored her svelte body, Priyanka reciprocated as she experienced new heights of ecstasy. Such kind of intense pleasure was new to both of them. That night, they surrendered to each other completely and slept peacefully in each other's arms.

After enjoying a hearty breakfast in the morning, they took the sightseeing trip arranged by the hotel.

Macau was a quaint place! Priyanka thought as she took the streets. During the day, they were silent but it came alive in the night, taking lively hues. They visited the Ruins of St. Paul's, the A-Ma temple from where Macau gets its name. They also went to Monte Forte where they took many pictures. Soon it was time to catch the afternoon ferry to Hong Kong.

The Hong Kong hotel in Kowloon was a complete contrast to the Venetian. The room was so tiny that they had to cuddle up to sleep.

While they were in Hong Kong, they did sightseeing in the day and passionate lovemaking at night. They even took the tram up to Victoria Peak –the highest hill on the island and enjoyed the panoramic view from there. The laser show at the waterfront in the evening was a spectacular sight too.

After sighing at the upmarket Central malls, they went to the street market and shopped as much as they could. The night market was another attraction. Getting gifts for the entire family was a big task but Priyanka enjoyed doing so. Disneyland surpassed their expectations. They both felt like naughty kids as they explored the vast wonderland.

Varun felt blissful as Priyanka seemed to be the perfect, doting wife, happily hanging on to his every word. Priyanka also felt overjoyed at the way her life was changing. Varun was everything and more she could have hoped for!

It was with these happy thoughts that they reached the airport for the return journey. After settling down in their seats, she kept the passports securely in her handbag. Varun tried to tease her a little.

"Well, Mrs Chopra, we will have to change your name and address in the passport soon."

Priyanka became silent as she heard those words.

Change her surname! Who do that nowadays? That was such an old fashioned thing to do.

She was not going to do it. She hated the whole concept of giving up her individuality just on account of marriage.

"We will talk about it later. I have to discuss this with you," she voiced out her reservation. Wanting to enjoy the flight, she then kept quiet and settled down to relax. Varun didn't pay much heed to her statement.

❖

Upon reaching home, Varun and Priyanka got busy with unpacking. They had brought gifts for Varun's parents and Priyanka's family as well. Priyanka excitedly handed over their gifts to mummyji and papaji, as she had decided to call them. But somehow the gifts did not go down well with them. Mummyji voiced her displeasure loudly and said she expected something better than the fancy handbag. Much to Priyanka's surprise, she had guessed it was a cheap bag from the local market.

How was she able to evaluate imported stuff! Priyanka wondered. Papaji wasn't very happy either. He just gave the pair of T-shirts a cursory look and kept them away, saying that you could find better quality in India itself.

Varun knew better than to react, and ignored their response. But Priyanka fumed internally.

We had spent our money to buy those gifts. Then, how could mummyji and papaji grumble about them so openly? They had no sense of decency. At least, they could have pretended to like the gifts.

But she kept quiet. She would visit her family on the weekend and share her travel stories with them. No point talking to these people here. They would just find faults.

Varun resumed office a week after their arrival. Priyanka was more and more unclear if she wanted to pursue her career. She would now be alone in the house all day with her in-laws. It was still too early for any rapport to be built among them. Rather, there was mostly an uneasy silence prevailing between them, as if a storm was brewing.

Mummyji and papaji were conservative in their thinking. They wanted to maintain a healthy distance from their daughter-in-law. They were not happy with the wedding gifts too, but had kept quiet on that front.

Priyanka was not used to such a stifling atmosphere. She had been brought up in a friendly environment where parents were more like friends than taskmasters. She thought she would have the same situation at her new home. By temperament, she was not used to experiencing any authoritative behaviour. Her first reaction was to rebel. The incident at the wedding and now the gifts had affected her already. She decided to let some time pass before attempting to be friendly. An uneasy calm thus prevailed.

The storm didn't take too much time to arrive.

❖

The first day, after Varun and her father-in-law left for work, Priyanka returned to her room, feeling lazy. She then got ready in a new, sleeveless knee-length dress purchased from Hong Kong and called Shikha to exchange notes. Mummyji had prepared breakfast, as was her habit, but she now expected Priyanka to come and help her in the kitchen for lunch. There was a maid who came for cleaning, but all the cooking was done by mummyji herself. She naturally expected her new daughter-in-law to reduce her load now, especially since she had heard so much about her cooking skills. She had just been diagnosed with diabetes and felt fatigued easily. So, she called out to Priyanka and asked her to cut the vegetables.

As soon as she saw what Priyanka was wearing, she lost her temper, more out of shock because it was totally unexpected.

"What are you wearing? Do you not have common sense? What will papaji think? At least see that before you dress up in such fancy dresses," she said, scolding Priyanka.

Priyanka was taken aback. She hadn't expected such a strong reaction. Actually, she had put on the dress without giving it much thought. According to her, there was nothing wrong in wearing something like this. At her parent's home, she would often wear shorts and no one said anything. And her father-in-law had left for his office and would be back only in the evening. So what was mummyji talking about?

"Go and change into a salwar-suit. Be decent. These dresses won't be allowed in my house."

Your house? And where is my house? Astounded, she came back to her room almost in tears. No one had ever shouted at her like this. Not even when she had come home from a party at 1 a.m., all dishevelled. This was not what she had expected. The old woman was a monster, she concluded. She was going to control even the smallest action in the house. *Her house*, not Priyanka's as she had declared.

She again decided to keep silent. Let Varun come in the evening. He will settle with mummyji. She was certain that Varun would understand and take her side. Seething with anger, she stayed in her room till the evening. Mummyji also didn't speak to her. Priyanka decided to skip lunch. Her hunger had disappeared. The breakfast had been too heavy, anyway.

In the evening, papaji returned first. Mummyji told him what had happened. It was a small house and the walls were thin. Priyanka could hear every word being spoken. Not that mummyji was trying to lower her voice in any way.

Did that mean they had heard their entire love-making last night? Priyanka wondered. *Better be careful here.*

Papaji got upset but he told mummyji to not say anything to Varun yet. They would wait and see what happens. He did not want such issues to come between their relationship with their son. He hoped that Varun would be able to guide Priyanka so that she could follow their norms and respect their sensibilities. Priyanka heard everything, but continued to sulk. Though she changed in a salwar suit, she ignored mummyji and did not help in the kitchen.

When Varun came home, he could sense something was wrong but as everyone was silent, he too didn't say anything. Later, after dinner, as Varun and Priyanka went out for a stroll, he spoke to her.

"What is wrong? What happened? Everyone is silent and seem tense."

"Nothing," she replied sullenly.

"Come on, sweetheart, tell me. You were so chirpy when I left in the morning. And now, just look at you."

He squeezed her hand lovingly, but Priyanka withdrew her hand and didn't respond.

Later at night, in their bedroom, he asked Priyanka again. Holding her close, he tried to kiss her. But, Priyanka pushed him away. Varun got slightly annoyed but settled in the bed and waited for her.

To his surprise, Priyanka didn't change but slipped into the bed, wearing her salwar suit.

"What happened? Are you not changing? Come on! Wear those satin shorts which we bought in Hong Kong. You look so sweet in them," Varun cajoled.

Priyanka's reaction was a curt "No."

Varun then sat up and demanded to know what was wrong. Priyanka finally spoke.

"I am now starting to learn that there are many unwritten rules and regulations in this house. You never mentioned all that to me," she said and glared at him.

Varun was perplexed. He had never seen anyone so angry.

"What rules and regulations? We are in our bedroom. What does anything else have to do with changing clothes?"

"Take permission from your mother first," replied Priyanka viciously. "She will decide what I should wear. She said only salwar suits are allowed in *her* home. How can I wear shorts? What if she comes in and checks?"

"Don't be silly. Why will mummy come into our bedroom to check what you are wearing?"

"You are calling me silly. What about your mother..." Priyanka trailed off, just stopping herself in time before she said anything exceptionally offensive.

She narrated the morning incident to Varun. He didn't know how to react. He could sense that this would not be a rare incident, but a starting point for many such occurrences which are yet to come. It worried him. He tried to coax Priyanka to calm down.

"Look, sweetheart, they are like your parents too. There is no harm in respecting their wishes. Once they get to know you better, I am sure they will also make efforts to accommodate your desires. These are small issues. Please don't blow them out of proportion."

But she would have none of it. "I have been brought up in a different atmosphere. My dad or ma never put such restrictions. No one is so regressive nowadays." The argument continued.

Finally they slept, back to back, facing away from each other, for the first time since marriage.

❖

In the morning, Priyanka kept sleeping and Varun went to the kitchen to make tea. Upon hearing the sound of the utensils, mummyji came in immediately.

"Where is Priyanka?" she asked.

"She has a headache. It is okay, I'll make tea," Varun replied. "Please don't make the issue bigger, mummy. She is being childish, I know, but try to understand her. She expects a bit of freedom, that's all – the way she was treated earlier in her house."

"And what should we do? What about our expectations?" mummyji asked, annoyed with his response. She had assumed that Varun would take her side.

"Come and speak to your father and hear what he says."

"I will do that later. Let things cool down a little," Varun answered.

Actually, he didn't know what to do. He was stuck between his parents and Priyanka. It was the proverbial catch 22 situation. The funny thing was that neither of them was completely wrong. But neither of them was completely right either. He had just not envisaged such a situation and he could sense that it was going to continue.

He greeted Priyanka with tea. That made her mood a little better. Varun again asked her not to overreact on small issues and try to build a rapport with his parents.

As he hugged her, he said, "Promise me, you'll do your best. For my sake!" he insisted. Priyanka gave in and muttered in a small voice what Varun wanted to hear. He then got ready for office. Priyanka too got up, and made breakfast for all. It was a simple breakfast – just some grilled vegetable sandwiches and cornflakes, which didn't require too much cooking skills. Everyone was happy with her gesture and peace reigned in the house once again.

Priyanka decided to take a step back and avoid confrontation. Now was not the time for it, she knew. Varun had shown that he was quite attached to his parents and she would have to act smartly if she wanted to have her way.

Once the two men left, though both the women remained with each other, there was no further conflict. Priyanka helped in the kitchen to cook lunch, but remained in her room for the rest of the day. She even made tea in the afternoon for her mother-in-law, which appeased her a bit.

So when Varun and papaji returned from office, they found a slightly better atmosphere at home.

6

Seeds of Discord

Few days passed without any further issues and Varun heaved a sigh of relief. Though Priyanka did not wear shorts or sleeveless dresses again, she often wore jeans but mummyji forced herself to remain quiet for the sake of her son.

Priyanka decided to visit her parents and informed mummyji about it. Alka's first response was to prevent her from going as the first visit to the parents' house after marriage was supposed to happen after following some rituals. Priyanka sulked upon hearing this. "Well, when will I be able to go then?" she asked resentfully.

"I want to meet my parents and friends."

Mummyji said that she would see the auspicious time. While Varun would go to bring her back, someone from her parents' home must come to accompany her. Priyanka found all this very stifling. As a retort, she planned a visit with her college friends for the next day. Mummyji couldn't say no but she did not appreciate such outings too much. She decided to find out when she could send Priyanka off to her parents' home.

The next day, Priyanka left with Varun and caught the local towards her college. She and her friends still frequented the café near the college. She felt happy to be out, away from the controlling atmosphere of the home and the hawk eye of her mother-in-law.

At the cafe, everyone welcomed her. The girls crowded around, asking endless questions. *What was being married like? How was mother-in- law? How was the honeymoon? Did she gamble in Macau? What did she win? What all did she shop?*

They just went on and on.

Soon it was time to go back and Priyanka, having got the attention she wanted, returned home in a cheerful mood. She sensed mummyji would now expect her to be in the kitchen. Though she didn't feel like it, she went and started the preparations for dinner. She had painted such a rosy picture of her life in front of her friends.

Thank god, they could not see the reality!

❖

A sort of routine developed in her new home. She would get up as early as she could and make tea for herself and Varun. Mummyji would have already made tea for herself and papaji by then. Then, she would help mummyji for breakfast and tiffins for papaji and Varun. Thereafter, she would relax till lunch time before the household chores beckoned her again. She avoided much interaction with mummyji, and kept to herself in her free time. She knew she should take up a job if she didn't want such a mundane life. But as was her nature, she was feeling lazy in making those efforts.

One day, Varun told Priyanka to be ready to go to the registrar's office to get the marriage certificate. He had taken leave from his office for it. As they were leaving for the marriage registrar's office, papaji called out from behind, "Do the formalities of name change, also. Get the changed name included in the marriage certificate. Later, it is a lengthy process."

Varun nodded but Priyanka's expression changed. She had thought that the matter was already settled. She had subtly expressed that she was not ready for it. But now, Varun was taking her for granted. She had told him clearly that she wanted to discuss but he hadn't broached the topic again. But now, papaji too had just given the order without asking her views on such a sensitive subject. So as soon as they stepped out of the house, she spoke to Varun, aggressively.

"Did you ever think that I may not want to change my surname? I am happy with my name as it is," she said in a loud, shrill voice.

"But that's the norm," Varun replied. "I never thought this could be an issue."

"Well, you are wrong. I told you during the flight journey that we will discuss about this. My name is my identity. It reminds me of my parents. I am not going to give that up," Priyanka responded firmly and Varun knew another storm was brewing.

Varun didn't want a fight right then. For the time being, they would register the marriage without a name change. He decided to resolve the matter later on. There was no urgency. They finished the work for the marriage certificate quickly. Varun had called two friends from office as a witness. They were in a hurry to get back to office so they just signed the documents when their turn came and rushed off.

Varun had planned to go to a nearby mall for lunch. Though Priyanka was not keen, he insisted and the bright atmosphere of the mall cheered her up. Later, while having ice cream, together, she again told Varun that she would not change her surname.

"I won't do it. You should have discussed it with me before assuming that it is the norm." Varun kept his cool but wondered what he was going to do.

Back home, his father asked them if everything had gone well.

"Of course," replied Varun.

"And when will you get the certificate?"

"Probably in a week. It is all online now. We'll get a message when it is ready."

"Good. Formally welcome to the family, Mrs Priyanka Chopra," papaji said, jokingly.

Varun didn't know how to respond. Looking at his reluctance, Priyanka spoke up, "Papaji, I don't want to change my surname. These are old-fashioned things. Nobody follows them anymore."

Papaji felt hurt that his daughter-in-law could speak in such a manner to him. He looked at Varun who kept his head down and mumbled that he would talk to her. But Priyanka was in no mood to stop.

"You just assumed that I would change my name. I find it regressive to say the least. My surname is my parent's legacy and I will not change it. They have no son and I have to carry forward my family name."

Seeing Priyanka's mood, Varun thought it was best to move away. He said he wanted something from the bedroom and literally dragged her there. He made a feeble attempt to convince her, but she was beyond listening. Tired of arguing, Varun fell quiet and didn't talk much to her for the next few days. Priyanka felt the strain between them and tried to be extra loving to Varun, but to no avail. The issue stood like a wall between them.

Finally, Priyanka relented a bit and told Varun that she would add his surname to hers. Priyanka Malhotra Chopra was the most she could do in this regard. Varun eased up a bit on hearing this and went to have a talk with his parents. Priyanka felt a strong dislike towards her in-laws, first for creating this issue and then, causing a rift between Varun and her. She knew she would always bear this grudge.

Mummyji too, was feeling annoyed with her daughter-in-law for showing disapproval towards a socially accepted norm. She could not accept that a girl who looked so simple and homely was, in reality, quite stubborn and strong headed. She had thought that Priyanka was a timid girl who would follow her diktats obediently and not question her authority. But this girl was proving her wrong time and again. And as if on cue, another episode unfurled the very next day.

❖

"Priyanka, I need you to give me all the wedding jewellery for keeping safely in my locker," Mummyji told her in a commanding tone. "Varun and I will go to the bank on Saturday and do the needful. Thereafter, if you need anything to use, you can let me know and I will see what is to be done. In fact, I feel the precious jewellery should always be in the locker and you can make do with the artificial one. As it is, no one can spot the difference," she continued merrily, without realizing the effect her words were having on Priyanka.

Priyanka was puzzled. She thought it was sinister of mummyji to have an eye on her jewellery and ask her to part with it. Her parents had saved their hard-earned money to buy her a gold set of bangles and heavy earrings in trendy style. She wanted to keep it close to her. In her eyes, the locker in her Godrej almirah was safe enough. The diamond set given by her in- laws was a delicate piece. She was sure that it was not too expensive but she did not want to part with it. There was also a dainty mangalsutra.

She voiced her thoughts, "Mummyji, I do not agree with you. The jewellery is safe here. I want to able to wear it whenever I want. Going to bank requires planning and moreover as a newlywed, I am sure I will be required to wear it often. Then, why to do all that labour? After all, it does belong to me and I must decide how to keep it."

Mummyji couldn't believe her ears. Again, she had been defied. She could have never talked in this manner to her in-laws. Edged on by such thoughts, she insisted and almost scolded Priyanka for questioning her decision-making. Priyanka ultimately gave in but shared her resentment to Varun, who had no solutions.

❖

Mummyji's sister decided to visit them from Chandigarh, along with her husband. He was the same uncle who had created a ruckus at Priyanka's wedding. They were searching for a match for their daughter and were coming to meet a couple of prospective boys' families.

For Priyanka, this meant a postponement of her visit to her maiden home. Moreover, mummyji was very excited. She asked papaji to stock the fridge with chicken and mutton and called Priyanka to plan the menu for the upcoming days. When she mentioned chicken curry and rogan josh, Priyanka was aghast. She was a complete vegetarian by choice and had never touched meat, let alone cook it.

"Mummyji, I can't stand the smell of meat," she said.

Mummyji was taken aback. She had never thought about this issue till now.

"Beta, eating meat is a way of life for us. We don't cook regularly at home, but meat is almost compulsory in any special occasion. Didi and jijaji will feel that we haven't looked after them properly if there is no meat," she said.

"So what is to be done?" asked Priyanka, sounding very distressed. "I feel like puking at the very sight of it."

"Well, there is nothing to be done. You just have to get used to it. The entire family and relatives will not change their food habits just for you. It would be better if you quickly learn to cook non-veg food. You don't have to eat it, that's fine. No one will insist," mummyji replied firmly.

The stern rebuke reminded Priyanka of her parents' home again where she had been offered enough freedom to make her own choices. She had seen Varun enjoy chicken burgers, but he had never really said anything on this disparity between them.

"I am sorry, mummyji. I can't do it," Priyanka said assertively. "Even if I tried, I will not be able to cook meat. The thought itself is nauseating and the smell is unbearable. Please don't ask me to do this. In fact, I don't know how I will stay inside the house and bear the smell while you are cooking it."

Mummyji was stunned into silence. After a moment, Priyanka spoke again.

"I think I will go to my parents' house while they are visiting.

That will solve the problem. They can eat whatever they want and I will not be there to cause any problem."

"This can't be allowed. It will be a big insult to them and to us if you go away just to avoid them," replied mummyji.

Allowed? Priyanka thought to herself. *What am I – a child or their servant?* But she kept silent.

Mummyji again grumbled to papaji. This time he had a word with Priyanka.

"Look here, beta," he said in a firm tone. "You are the new entrant to our home. You are expected to change your ways of life, not us. It would augur well if you could be flexible and try to follow the instructions of your mother-in-law."

Though Priyanka wanted to give a rejoinder, she refrained. But she fought with Varun the whole night.

❖

"Why didn't you tell me all this before, Varun? You have not been transparent. And now your parents demand so much. Where is the happiness you promised me?" She broke down and started weeping.

Varun was now feeling equally trapped. He hadn't anticipated such issues. Priyanka had been such a sweet girl back then. Now she was being rigid on everything. She would have to adapt at least a bit. After all, he could not ask his parents to change their eating habits.

But before he could speak, Priyanka spoke again.

"And what is this 'my house' business? Both of them keep

saying it is *their* house. Tell me, do you have no say in anything here? Are you a paying guest? I want this to be our house where I have the freedom to eat, drink and wear what I like, not what someone else tells me to."

Varun was shocked at her ferocity. She was a totally changed person. Gone was the simple girl he thought he was marrying. Instead, she had become a self-centred person with myopic thinking. Even the six months they spent going out before marriage did not uncover these aspects.

"Priyanka, you must accommodate their habits. You never showed earlier that you could be so unyielding. Don't spoil the atmosphere of the house, please." He tried to calm her down but couldn't find any solution to the issue.

To save the crisis from getting worse, for the time being, Priyanka decided she would make an excuse and go out of the house when the meat was being cooked. She knew that the physical revulsion she had from the smell was something she couldn't handle. And she would pretend a headache during meal times. She wouldn't be able to eat, anyway, watching meat being devoured at the table.

7

Mausiji's Arrival

It was a Saturday and Varun spoke to his mother about Priyanka. Mausiji was arriving in the evening.

"Mummy, I think you should give more time to Priyanka. She is in a totally new environment. The change is too quick for her." His father overheard him and intervened.

"It would be better if you ask Priyanka to adjust quickly. She is the daughter-in-law and she must adjust to our ways. Did her parents not teach her that? It's very strange how they have brought her up. You should firmly tell her to change. Should we change our lifestyle now, at this stage of our lives? I have started feeling that we should have got you married to someone from a similar background so that these issues did not arise." Varun stopped him from continuing further.

"Papa, there is no point of talking about this. The past events cannot be reversed now. You have to see her situation also."

Priyanka heard all this and was aghast.

Varun's decision to marry me is a mistake according to them!

Her mood soured further. She stayed in her room the whole day. Varun did not say anything to her. He knew she would react violently to anything he said.

❖

In the evening, Varun came to the room and started cleaning it. He cleared up their clothes and removed their stuff from the bathroom.

"What are you doing"? Priyanka asked, suddenly afraid. *Was he walking out of the house?*

"Mausiji and mausaji will be using this room. We will be in the drawing-room till they are with us," Varun explained.

"What?" Priyanka asked. "Now I have to vacate my room also?" It was ironic how, in a few weeks, she had started to think of the house as her own but she had not developed any such feelings for the people in the house.

"Well, Priyanka, that has always been the norm with us. If any guest comes, I give my room to them. It is a basic courtesy. And mausaji has a back problem and we can't expect him to sleep on a mattress on the floor."

"That was earlier. You were not married then. Things have to change now. They can sleep in your parents' room if they are so keen to extend this kind of welcome," Priyanka responded insolently.

Varun was annoyed. "Why are you so selfish all the time? It should be your duty to take care of the guests and my parents. But you are very uncaring. You have to bend and compromise to maintain relationships. You can't have your way on each and every issue. Learn to care for others and their feelings."

"And who will take care of me and my feelings? You?" Priyanka retorted, almost rudely.

Varun did not respond and left the room. Priyanka felt terrible. This was not how she had imagined her married life to be. Even the elementary freedoms were being denied to her. She was expected to be docile and sacrificing in the name of 'adjustments'. Varun too, was not on her side. He had conveniently forgotten about the wedding incident when he created a scene and no one had said anything to this uncle. Instead, all hospitality and generosity was being extended to him.

Priyanka remained gloomy for the rest of the day. She spoke to her mother on the phone and shared her unhappiness with her. Ma, who had always apprehended such issues, told her to be patient and cooperative. She advised that she should try to win over her in-laws. This upset Priyanka even further and she felt that no one in the world understood her plight.

❖

When the guests arrived, Priyanka greeted them with a *namaste* but did not touch their feet. Only when mummyji asked her, did she perform the gesture perfunctorily. Mummyji glared at her as she did it.

Fortunately for Priyanka, mausiji said they had already eaten on the way and were not hungry. So, the meat was avoided.

"We'll miss the delicious food Priyanka would have made for us. We'll try it tomorrow. Mausaji's back is hurting due to the journey and he wants to lie down now," said mausiji.

Priyanka couldn't stop her blunt response.

"No, Mausiji. I did not cook dinner. I am a vegetarian. I can't stand the sight of meat being cooked. I feel nauseated by the smell."

Mausiji was surprised at the rude reply. Later she asked her sister about it. Mummyji confided in her about Priyanka's unbecoming behaviour. Mausiji sympathised with her.

"I had feared something like this from the beginning itself. The whole family appeared cunning to me. I will counsel Priyanka whenever I get the opportunity. You have to remain strict from the beginning itself. Otherwise these young girls will never adjust."

In the morning as Priyanka made tea, mausiji descended upon her and started advising her about how to be a good daughter- in- law. Priyanka ignored her and went about her work.

"She is a hard nut to crack. You are in for a tough time. Look at her – neither good looks nor from a high family, yet having such an attitude," mausiji told mummyji.

Mummyji nodded and moaned about her bad destiny.

Mausiji and her ever-complaining husband left after three days, having successfully finalised the match. Fortunately, all their dinners were outside and Priyanka somehow managed to stay out of the kitchen during the lunch preparations. She was simply waiting to have her room and privacy back.

Before leaving, mausiji invited the boy's side over to Chandigarh to meet the girl.

"This is how marriages should happen," was her parting remark to her sister, adding further fuel to fire. Mummyji again cribbed to Varun about marrying Priyanka in haste.

Though Varun did not usually like hearing negative things about Priyanka, this time he tended to agree. Priyanka's behaviour had been abominable. He hoped she would revert to her simple, old self, the way he had known her before marriage.

❖

The strained atmosphere in the house continued after mausiji's departure. Obviously, it affected the relationship between Priyanka and Varun. Priyanka tried to normalise things between them by trying to make love to Varun, but he was not in that frame of mind. Priyanka felt a strong dislike towards her in-laws. She blamed them for everything that was going wrong.

Meanwhile, Priyanka's father called papaji and requested to allow her to come and visit them for a few days. This ritual of the girl going back to her father's house was usually performed a few days after the marriage ceremony, but had been left pending. Papaji usually never said no to anyone and mummyji had also figured out an auspicious time. So it was agreed that dad would come on Sunday and take Priyanka home for some days. Priyanka was fed up of her situation anyway and she thought it was best if she went away for some time to get some space from her in-laws.

It will do them all some good! She thought. So she packed her bags happily for her maiden visit to her home after marriage. She intended to stay there for a week. She thought she would also use this time to work out her career prospects and see if she could enrol for a short term course in office management and administration.

❖

Dad's visit on Sunday was without any unnecessary stress and drama. For a moment, the fleeting thought that mummyji might open Pandora's box and start cribbing against her, had occurred to Priyanka. But thankfully, nothing like that happened. He stayed for a very short time.

Varun, mummyji and papaji were courteous and offered him tea and snacks. But dad politely excused himself, under the cover of the traditional norm that the girl's parents should not have even a glass of water in the girl's in-laws' house. Priyanka was all packed up and ready and she left after saying a brief goodbye. She felt relieved upon reaching Borivali. Her parents were also delighted. Both asked her if she was happy. She nodded and smiled so that they could feel reassured. She did not want to burden them from the moment of her arrival. She felt like asking her mother if she had faced similar issues. And if so, how she had overcome them. As far as she could recall, her mother had a loving relationship with her grandparents. But then, her mother was not very individualistic and would have surrendered to their demands easily.

Brushing her thoughts aside, she brought out the gifts from their trip abroad for them and for a moment, forgot her despair amid the excitement shown, especially by Shikha and Sapna. Both also listened with mouths gaping about the details from her Hong Kong and Macau trip. Priyanka enjoyed all the attention and she also enjoyed ma's sumptuous cooking after such a long time. She felt free and relaxed.

The next day, she confided in her parents about the issues faced by her. Both were very upset but had different reasons. Ma immediately started blaming dad for everything – from spoiling Priyanka since she was a child to fixing up the match with an unknown family. Dad was more worked up about the fact that his beloved daughter was facing troubles. He told Priyanka that he did not mind talking to either her father-in-law or Varun about it, but he did not want to spoil things further. Things were still not beyond repair. There was no doubt that Priyanka must adjust in her in-laws' home now and keep Varun on her side.

"To get something, you have to give first. You have to be patient and accommodating. Always look at the bigger picture in life. Try to win their hearts, beta. I am sure you will succeed," he said wisely and asked Priyanka to give time to her fledgling relationships.

Priyanka was not too happy upon hearing this sermon but pondered over it for the next few days. Shikha and Sapna kept her mood buoyant. She confided a bit in Shikha too about her travails. Shikha gave a very different perspective.

"Didi, you can't be submissive. How can they impose restrictions on you? Dad and ma have never ever interfered in any of our decisions. And how can jiju not support you? After all, he is your husband. That is why I am not in favour of an arranged marriage," she stated grandly. Priyanka was all the more convinced that she had a boyfriend tucked away somewhere.

She thought about the two contrasting suggestions she had received. In her heart she wanted to follow what Shikha was saying but her mind told her that the reality was different. Varun would never question his parents' unrealistic expectations. And she needed Varun in her life.

She decided she must win over Varun but at the same time, she must tackle her in-laws, without appearing offensive. Her main objective should be to find happiness with Varun. She also thought that taking up a job would be a solution. She would have her own money and would gain reprieve from the controlling in-laws as well. Therefore, she aggressively searched for correspondence courses in office administration. To her delight, she found one that suited her in the Mumbai Open University and she happily filled out the form, meaning to tell Varun later.

❖

The week passed by quickly. Soon she started missing Varun. When Varun came to take her back, she greeted him warmly.

He stayed for some time, chatting with her parents and sisters before taking leave, saying he had to be home before dinner.

On the journey back, Priyanka clung to Varun and asked how he had been. She told him how much she had missed him. Varun had also missed the cosiness of being with her. While they were apart, he had thought about all the past conflicts. Even though, he felt that it was Priyanka's fault, he had asked his parents to be more accommodative towards her.

As the auto raced towards Varun's home, both hoped in their hearts that this was the start of a more nurturing relationship.

8

When Hospital Called

It was payday which made Varun feel very excited. He had been thinking of a small weekend trip with Priyanka to a resort in Alibag. It would help them to come closer. Priyanka too was eagerly waiting for Varun to get his salary and do some shopping for herself.

Varun's money was all handled by his mother. She operated his salary account. If he needed money for anything, he would ask her for it. He thought that it was perfectly natural to do so. So upon reaching home, he told mummyji that the salary had been credited in his account and he would need fifteen thousand for the trip.

Priyanka overheard him and couldn't believe her ears. She went to Varun and asked him loudly, "did you get your salary today? I need around ten-thousand rupees for some shopping." Her way of speaking angered mummyji and she immediately scolded her.

"Look, Priyanka, this is no way to behave. We have to look at all the expenses of the house. You can't keep indulging yourself and demand like this. I expected Varun to have already told you about the way we run our house." After completing her statement, she looked at Varun with anticipation.

A helpless expression came on Varun's face. He wished Priyanka was not so impulsive. He started speaking to Priyanka but she marched off to the bedroom, fuming. Varun followed her and found her sulking as he entered the bedroom. He wanted to tell her about the trip to Alibag that he was planning. But her surly mood made him hold on.

"Priyanka, come on, you should not have just blurted out like that. I wish you had spoken to me first, I would have explained everything." Varun said. "Now things have again become tense."

"It's not my fault," Priyanka replied tersely, applying moisturiser to her face with angry strokes. "And first I want to ask you. Am I not your wife?"

Varun was flabbergasted. He could sense where things would head and again told Priyanka to just calm down first.

"Answer me first," Priyanka almost yelled, pulling at his collar.

Varun kept his cool and answered her, "Yes, of course, you are my wife. You are my priority."

"Then how come you give your salary to your mother? And on top of that, I can't even get my due if I want to spend," Priyanka demanded.

Varun was silent. This was going to get bad, he knew. Priyanka continued her tirade.

"I was waiting so eagerly for your first salary after marriage. You should know that I have the foremost right over your money, but you simply hand it over to your mother. You are not a bachelor anymore and I don't want my husband to be so gullible."

She paused for breath. Varun was stunned. He had never thought that this could be such a venomous issue. He tried to placate her again.

"Please try to understand. Papa and mummy are our parents. I give them my salary as a token of my respect. And they will never say no to any of our expenses. We are a small family and these issues should not crop up between us. Look, I was planning a trip to Alibag together. They were very happy when I told them about it."

"What trip? So they know about the trip, but I don't?" Priyanka again lashed out accusingly. "Moreover, didn't she just refuse to give what I had asked, can you explain that?"

Varun got exasperated. "It's becoming impossible to please you, Priyanka. You just think about yourself all the time."

"And you think only of your parents," Priyanka countered.

After this intense fight, the trip to Alibag was obviously off. Priyanka kept fretting all through the next days and tried to convince Varun that her point of view was correct. Varun was in no mood to listen to her constant complaints and firmly told her that she needed to change her mindset and start thinking of the entire family as one unit.

Then, Varun went on an official tour to Pune and returned after four days. Priyanka called him many times but Varun did not respond. When he came back, he was taciturn and stayed silent most of the time.

Varun's cold behaviour shook Priyanka a bit. She remembered her dad's advice and her own resolution. She needed to make sure that Varun was on her side. So outwardly, she tried to remain civil with her in-laws. She knew that she should not cold shoulder them totally. That would only incense Varun and worsen things further. Inwardly, her negative feelings towards mummyji and papaji solidified. They were the root cause of her troubles.

Besides, she resolved to get a job. The course which she had joined had started. It was six months long and she knew she would start looking for jobs before it ended.

Two more days passed in this manner. On the third day, as Priyanka was preparing to go to sleep, her phone rang. It was her mother. Dad had collapsed with a heart attack. The neighbours had rushed him to a nearby hospital but his condition was serious. Ma was distraught.

"Just come to the hospital!" ma told Priyanka frantically.

Emerging white-faced, she gave the information to Varun and then, looked at him. Varun lost no time to respond.

"Let's leave immediately," he said and got ready in just a minute. After telling his parents, both of them rushed to the hospital.

❖

It was nearly 10 p.m. and there was little traffic on the roads. It still took them half an hour to reach. Both ma and Shikha were outside. Dad was in ICU and the doctors were performing some tests. They would know the situation soon.

The doctor came out from the ICU and gave them a briefing. He said that dad had a heart attack due to a blocked artery. He showed them the angiography report which showed an artery that was almost 80 percent blocked. He said that while they had managed to stabilize the vital parameters, he strongly recommended an angioplasty immediately to put a life-saving stent.

Priyanka had heard about the overuse of stents and wanted to take a second opinion. But the other three overruled her. They said it was best to go with the doctor's advice. Fortunately, dad had medical insurance and they just had to show the identification card. They didn't have to pay any money right then. Varun acted swiftly and completed the necessary formalities. Priyanka was in a daze and could barely console her mother.

Thankfully, the procedure was successfully done and the doctor told them that dad would be in the hospital under observation for the next forty-eight hours. He was under sedation and they would be able to meet him in the morning.

Priyanka wanted to stay in the hospital and refused to move from there, just in case dad woke up and needed something. Varun then dropped ma and Shikha home in Borivali and then went back to his own home.

❖

The next morning, Varun and his parents visited the hospital. Papaji told Priyanka to take care of her dad and be with her mother. Inspite of everything that had happened, Priyanka was touched by their concern.

Maybe I have misunderstood them. She thought. She, along with Shikha, took turns to be at the hospital while Sapna and ma managed the home. Varun was most considerate and kept constantly in touch with Priyanka. He even reassured her over finances and said that he'll take care of any contingency.

Dad was home after three days. Though the doctor said he should resume his normal life as soon as possible, he still needed a lot of care. Shikha's exams were round the corner. Priyanka wanted to be with her father and support her mother. She told Varun that it was her duty to help her parents at this time. Ma, however was hesitant. She said that Priyanka should go back to her home and take care of Varun and her in-laws.

❖

After a few days, mummyji spoke to Priyanka. Mausiji's daughter's wedding was coming up. She wanted Priyanka to travel with them to Chandigarh. She said that it would be very awkward for them in the family if their newly wed daughter-in-law was not with them in such an important family function. Especially now that her father was back from the hospital, they had no excuse.

"But it is your decision," mummyji added. "You have to decide what your priorities are. I have explained the situation, but I will not insist on anything. You decide what is the right thing to do."

Priyanka felt highly pressurized. On the face of it, it was her decision. So her in-laws couldn't be criticised about their behaviour. But mummyji had made it very clear what she expected her to do.

How can I leave my father at such a critical time? She thought.

What if dad has a problem again while I am enjoying the wedding at Chandigarh? I will never be able to forgive myself. And ma needs me. She is being brave, but she is still under shock. Shikha is busy with her exams. Sapna can do very little in terms of providing care. Ma needs emotional support at this time. Otherwise she may break down. The marriage will happen, anyway, even without me. In fact, things will be better if I am not there in Chandigarh. They will expect me to follow some tradition or the other, of which I may know nothing about, and then criticize me for not following it. So, she finally decided to stay away.

So Priyanka told mummyji that she would not be able to go to Chandigarh with them. She explained her thought process to

Varun as nicely as she could. Varun could see the situation from both sides and felt he was caught in between. He tried to make an attempt to persuade Priyanka, anyway.

"Chandigarh is less than three hours away by flight. If there is a problem here, we can rush down immediately," he told Priyanka.

"And will you guarantee there won't be any social problems at Chandigarh? I do not know much about your family traditions and I do not want mummyji to go ballistic at me."

"I'll be with you all the time. I will cover for you, Priyanka!"

"Don't make promises you know you can't keep, Varun. All the women will be together. The men will be separate. You won't even know what mess would happen and where."

Varun gave up. It was a valid point to an extent. He also knew all hell would break loose if couldn't protect her.

So Priyanka stayed in Mumbai and there was nothing he could do except listen to his mother's taunts.

❖

Gradually dad's health improved but Priyanka's relationship with her in- laws deteriorated.

Ma sensed the friction and urged Priyanka to go back. She thanked Varun profusely for being supportive and letting Priyanka stay with her during their hour of need. Dad too appreciated the prompt help by Varun. He had tears in his eyes as he thanked Varun for all his help.

Varun actually wanted to ask him to tell Priyanka to behave a little better with his parents. But, he could not find the right words, especially taking into account dad's heart attack and health.

Priyanka returned with Varun to her home with a heavy heart. She knew she had to face her mother-in-law's jibes but was still shaken by her father's illness and remained quiet. She had no will to fight anymore. She also knew that Varun had been a saviour at the hospital and decided she would not fight with him on any issue.

❖

After Priyanka's dad recovered, he made up his mind to quit his job and leave the hustle bustle of Mumbai. He wanted to go back to Ambala and live a quiet life there.

Shikha could finish her studies in Mumbai and stay in a PG and Sapna would be with them. He was sure he would find a suitable job there. Priyanka was not very happy with this decision but she knew her father really wanted it. She thought that Shikha could stay with them rather than in a PG. She asked Varun about it who in turn asked his parents. His parents refused outright saying their house was too small to accommodate Shikha. But the main reason was that they didn't want to take the responsibility of a young girl. They didn't know how to handle these 'modern' girls. Priyanka was enough for them.

Priyanka knew all this for she could hear the whole discussion in the small house with thin walls. She still felt that they could have tried a little to understand her feelings and attempted to come up with a solution. Their house was rented. They could have probably moved to a larger house. Once she got a job, she too would have helped financially. And Shikha would be her responsibility, not theirs. But as she had decided, she remained quiet, though her heart was full of dislike towards them.

9

Bigger House Needed

Two years passed by. There had been a lot of friction and bickering between Priyanka and her in-laws. The issues remained the same. There were differences due to eating habits, dressing style and even daily routine. Both sides were divided on all issues and Varun was always being forced to validate one or the other.

The biggest change was that Priyanka found a job and had started working. But that too had turned up into quite an issue with everyone.

Due to dad's heart attack and other issues, she had completely forgotten to share about her course with Varun, mummyji and papaji. Varun discovered her notes by chance one day and was utterly surprised. She shared her aim of taking up a job. Though he did not mind, he became upset at the fact that Priyanka had not shared such a big development with him.

"How could you have not told me? It shows you are still not emotionally connected with us." He was very annoyed. He also told Priyanka to keep mummyji and papaji included in all her decisions but Priyanka did not pay heed.

"I will cross that bridge when I come to it. It's not as if they will support me. The course is about to finish and I have to think of the exams."

The short course finished soon. Priyanka cleared the exams too and she immediately registered on a job portal. Within a month, she got an offer from a tech start up and though the salary was not that high, she was in such a hurry to step out of the house that she agreed to take it.

Mummyji did not welcome her decision. She openly told her that she should have consulted them first. Moreover, she was developing health issues and it was high time that she 'retired' from the kitchen and Priyanka took full responsibility for it. Papaji was, in principle, not against her working but he also felt offended by merely being informed about such an important decision.

❖

Priyanka started her job just as her marriage was turning a year old. She decided not to be affected by her in-laws' reaction. They were not really interested in her progress. Her parents were happy and that was what really mattered.

Her new routine started and she knew she would have to do her share of chores if she was to find peace with mummyji.

For household work, there was an informal division of who would do what. Priyanka would make the tea and breakfast in the morning for everyone before she left for office. She would make a simple lunch too and pack all the tiffins.

Then, mummyji had to make chapattis for herself later in the day. The cleaning maid came in after she had left for office and mummyji would supervise her work. Initially, mummyji expected her to help with dinner too. But Priyanka felt tired in the evening and wanted to unwind. She soon found a way out. She deliberately left office late in order to avoid cooking dinner. By the time she would reach home, mummyji would have started dinner preparation. Staying late also earned her the 'hardworking' tag in office, so it worked well both ways.

Besides, neither papaji nor mummyji was a fan of her cooking. So Priyanka thought it was best to let mummyji be the 'lord of the kitchen' and relax a little after a hectic day in the office. She had no desire to be overzealous. She realized that somewhere at the back of her mind, mummyji didn't want to let go off her powerful position. Mummyji loved the fact that everyone depended on her for the house to run smoothly.

Priyanka enjoyed her office environment and quickly made friends. Rita, the data analyst and Adil, the financial adviser were in the same age group. They often enjoyed their lunches together. They even made plans for weekend outings but to buy peace at home, Priyanka refused to join.

This peace however was only on the surface. Underneath, there was always a simmering issue. Mummyji would even grumble aloud that Priyanka hardly went to her parents' house in Ambala as that would give her some reprieve from Priyanka's behaviour. Though she did not say much to her directly, Priyanka could easily overhear when she spoke to papaji or Varun. She obviously felt hurt by these remarks. She missed her parents, especially in such situations. Shikha had finished her studies and joined them in Ambala. She had started working as a school teacher there. She wanted to do Ph.D later.

Priyanka often wished she could go back to the carefree life that she had lived earlier. The daily stressful atmosphere in the house started to get to her. For Varun's sake, she tried her best to stay aloof from mummyji and not retaliate strongly against her comments. However, the fact of their staying together was a big detriment to her happiness. According to her, mummyji and papaji were the source of all disputes. Keeping all these feelings pent up inside made her silent and gloomy most of the time. Varun too was affected by the atmosphere in the house. Caught in the quagmire, he also started spending more time in the office as an excuse to stay away from home. Thus, he could focus more on his job and work hard.

This brought an unexpected result. Varun's dedication was rewarded in the form of an early promotion. He was made an area manager and had to travel regularly to supervise the medical representatives in his territory for increasing sales. He liked the freedom which travelling gave him and the relief from the stifling atmosphere at home. Initially he had tried to resolve things by speaking to both Priyanka and his parents, but eventually gave up as he saw that neither Priyanka nor his parents were willing to compromise. So now, he just preferred to stay away.

❖

As the monsoons set in, mummyji caught the flu and had fever. Varun was busy in office and was able to spend only a short time in the evenings with her. Priyanka had to bear the responsibility of nursing her. She hated the extra burden. She took two days off from her office and tried to take care of her.

Though Alka was ill, she expressed a desire to eat hot khichdi or daliya for each meal. Priyanka did the needful but with a disdainful attitude.

One evening, she caught mummyji speaking against her to papaji. "This girl can't even make good khichdi," she grumbled. The next day Priyanka confronted her. "How can you speak ill of me when I am taking care of you!"

"Everything I want is a burden to you. Will you treat your own mother like this?"

This annoyed Priyanka to no end and she just left for office in a huff, without doing any cooking. For the whole day, she was in an acrid mood, not speaking properly to her colleagues. She knew what to expect when she returned home. And sure enough, papaji scolded her in the evening.

"How could you just walk off? Alka had to fend for herself in the day. You know she has fever, yet you could not keep patience.

It's shameful. I am slowly starting to think that you and Varun should search for a new home and stay separately."

Priyanka was secretly delighted to hear this but mummyji refused to hear anything further. Papaji extracted an apology out of her and before Varun came, some normalcy was restored in the house. Priyanka continued to feel miserable.

❖

One evening, finding Varun close to her after many weeks, mummyji held his hand and made him sit next to her.

"Beta, I feel bad about many things, but you see Priyanka never tries to adjust with us," she said slowly.

"Mummy, let it be now. There is no point to discuss all this," Varun replied, slightly irritated. He didn't want to start the endless complaints again. He accepted the fact that his mother and his wife would continue to be at loggerheads perpetually.

"There is definitely one point," Mummyji continued undeterred. "I feel that the problems can be greatly reduced if Priyanka starts to think of herself as our own. And that is possible if there is a child to bind her to this family. It's been two years since your marriage. I hope you understand what I mean."

Varun smiled but kept silent. The thought had come to him also but expecting a negative reaction from Priyanka, he had kept quiet. He told his mother to be patient.

"You know her well by now, mummy. Let her decide for herself. You can't force her into doing anything."

"Yes, but at least you could start talking. Who knows..." Mummyji trailed off wistfully.

❖

In the bedroom, later that night, he hugged Priyanka from behind. Surprised, she asked him what was wrong.

"Nothing, just loving you," Varun replied naughtily and they indulged in passionate love making. Varun wondered if Priyanka would possibly conceive after such a steamy act and drifted off to sleep with those thoughts.

Priyanka, however, had no such plans. She did not want any additional responsibility at this stage. She was already fed up of the situation at home and a baby, would further add to her woes. She had started taking contraceptive pills without telling anyone and she was happy to wait for motherhood.

Mummyji soon got better but the thought of having a grandchild stayed with her. She now started nagging Priyanka almost on a daily basis.

"Look, all things are good if they happen in a timely manner," she would say. "Varun is our only child because I too made the mistake of having a child late and then, could not have another one. So please, Priyanka, start thinking in terms of expanding your family. A baby brings good luck and blessings from the forefathers." She tried to coax Priyanka.

Priyanka felt awkward discussing all this so directly. She kept quiet initially but one day she just burst out.

"Mummyji, these are very personal decisions. You should not interfere in all this. When the time is right, the baby will come. As of now, where is the time to even think of adding to the family? I come back so tired from the office. After that, I'm always occupied with house chores. Varun is always travelling and for the atmosphere of the house, let's not talk about it in detail."

After a pause, she continued, "Moreover, where is the space for an extra person in this house? Already, we have to move out of our room when anyone visits. We could not accommodate Shikha, though I wanted her to stay here. How will we adjust when there is a child?"

Mummyji became silent after this outburst as she knew that Priyanka would not pay any heed to her words. But she continued to mention it to Varun whenever she could.

❖

One Saturday, Varun was at home and he thought it would be nice to go out for dinner with Priyanka. It seemed ages since they had gone out together. The rains had put him in a romantic mood. Priyanka agreed immediately. She was only too happy to get out of the house.

Earlier, whenever she proposed to go out, Varun always wanted to go as a family and take mummyji and papaji along. But Priyanka didn't enjoy these outings. Both parents were too awkward the whole time. They had too many restrictions about the kind of food they would eat and complained about wasting money by paying so much to the restaurant for such ordinary food. So after a few times, they stopped going out.

But this time, it would be just the two of them.

Varun decided to splurge. They took a cab and went to a plush restaurant in the neighbourhood. Varun decided to make the most of Priyanka's happy mood. Over dinner, he broached the topic of parenthood.

"Sweetheart, let's think in terms of a baby now," he said.

Priyanka kept her spoon down and said aggressively, "Oh, so mummyji has been manipulating you on this issue. Why can't she leave us alone? And why our lives should be so controlled by your parents? I don't understand."

As usual, Varun told her to calm down. "This has nothing to do with what mummy may or may not say. It's my desire and you should also feel the same by now."

Not wanting to spoil her evening further, Priyanka kept quiet but inside she was seething with anger. Her mother-in-law had again succeeded in creating an issue. She wondered when she was going to be free of them. She wondered if Varun could get a transfer to another city. Papaji would never leave the city and nor would mummyji. And she could easily get another job in another city.

The issue remained hanging between them and Priyanka took her pills regularly with even more zeal.

❖

Soon it was time for her father-in-law's retirement and Varun started planning a party to mark the event.

He booked a banquet hall and asked Priyanka to buy new clothes for the entire family. She was also supposed to help him in deciding the décor and the menu. Some of his excitement rubbed off on Priyanka also and she got involved in making the arrangements. She went shopping for clothes, but remembering the honeymoon gift fiasco, this time she sent pictures of the clothes on Whatsapp to mummyji and asked her to choose. The whole thing took a long time and the shopkeeper almost lost patience, but at least there was peace at home.

Priyanka also asked her parents to join them for the function but dad wanted to avoid travel. Shikha came over a weekend before the event and the two sisters were very happy to meet and catch up. Shikha was doing well as a teacher and seemed to be in no hurry to get married. Priyanka envied her carefree life.

"Didi, you haven't visited us even once. Ma and dad miss you," Shikha said forcefully. Priyanka promised to visit Ambala soon.

The retirement day arrived, bright and sunny. They even went to papaji"s office to attend the function there. In the evening, they reached the venue and in time, the guests poured in. The party was a big success. Everyone appreciated the décor and the menu. Varun felt emotional as they were returning to their house. He told Priyanka that he still had hope that they could all live together happily. All he wanted was that his parents should be comfortable especially now that they were senior citizens. Priyanka could barely nod.

❖

A few days later, papaji summoned them to the drawing room to discuss an important matter.

"I wanted to give all this retirement money to you to buy a flat and settle down in Mumbai," he said to Varun. "You will be starting a family, soon. This flat is too small. We need a larger one."

"But what is the need, papa? We have been staying happily in this flat for so long. The owner can't throw us out."

"Look at your job. You have to be in Mumbai. You are a senior manager now, based in head office. Very few large companies have their head offices outside Mumbai. Even those which do, the seniors always sit in Mumbai. And when you have children, you will need more space, anyway. Your mother and I have decided to go back to Chandigarh to our ancestral house. We will pass our *vanaprastha* years more peacefully there."

Varun was reluctant about the money and totally against the idea of his parents shifting to Chandigarh.

"The money belongs to you," he replied. "You have worked so hard to save it. Now it is your time to enjoy spending it. It is my duty to take care of my old parents. You are not shifting anywhere. How could you even think like that? You have already done more than enough. I can take a loan to buy a flat, if required."

Priyanka scowled at him as he said this. She had an emotional reaction to every matter related to money. Having grown up in an environment where it was always short, she had this urge to always acquire more. Seeing Varun refuse such a lucrative offer made her very furious. One of her dreams was to have a house in her own name. After buying a car, of course! In fact, she thought, her in-laws should give them the flat here and go to Chandigarh as they had decided. That would work out so much better. Instead of buying a house, they can spend the money on themselves. So while the conversation was not conclusive, Priyanka's thoughts started flying in that direction. After a lot of thought, she decided that buying a house in her name was a better idea. It would be the first major asset she owned. She felt good by just imagining that.

She started to goad Varun into agreeing to do what papaji wanted to do. Once they had their own flat, they would save the rental money and then, perhaps they could have a baby too. She kept on harping on these lines till Varun agreed with her – more to get her off his back than because he was convinced. He told his father that they would try to buy the flat they were living in from the owner even if it was small. Or else, they would look for a similar one in the neighbourhood. They needed a bigger house but it was not possible for them to purchase it due to budget issues. Along with his father's money, he would invest Priyanka's and his own savings and take a loan for the balance. However, Chandigarh was out of the question, he concluded.

Priyanka heaved a sigh of relief as having a bigger house really mattered to her and finally harmony prevailed in the house. But the peace was short-lived.

❖

While the negotiations with the owner of the house they were living in were in progress, one day, over dinner, papaji announced that the flat would be bought in mummyji's name. Varun also nodded as if it was the obvious thing to do. Priyanka was stunned. She felt as if her heart had stopped beating for a moment. She could see her dream of having a house in her own name vanishing.

Since she tried not to disagree with her in-laws openly and especially in front of Varun, she kept quiet on the dinner table. But later, in their bedroom, she virtually attacked Varun.

"How could you possibly agree to something like this? The flat should be in our name. You have to resist this," she said forcefully.

Varun was shocked.

"Be in your senses, Priyanka. I can never speak like that to my parents. How does the name matter? We are all one family. I don't know how and when you will appreciate this fact."

"If the name doesn't matter, why is papaji insisting on mummyji's name? And why did mummyji insist to keep all my jewellery in her locker. You have never understood my insecurities. You are blinded by their views," Priyanka yelled.

"Because that is how it has always been done here. Even the rent agreement is in mummy's name. Parents' always mean well for their children. And see, I am the only child. Everything is ours, anyway. It will all come to us, eventually. So what's your problem?"

The argument continued, but this time Varun was firm. He told Priyanka to stop thinking about these silly notions and focus on taking care of papaji and mummyji. She was aghast upon hearing Varun speak like this. She just started crying. She couldn't find the right words to explain to Varun how she felt about her most treasured dream crumbling, how insecure and alone she felt. At such moments she wished she had her parents to turn to, especially her dad. He would have given her a big hug and set things right. But now, they were far away in Ambala. Somehow, talking on the phone wasn't the same. She wanted to be loved and comforted.

Inspite of her best efforts, the issues with her in-laws were affecting her relationship with Varun. She had not achieved what she had dreamt of when she got married to Varun. But now that she was married, she was stuck. She couldn't get out. The thought made her restless. Her in-laws had become her biggest hurdle in her happiness.

10

New Year Party

The process of buying the flat gave no pleasure to Priyanka now. She felt that Varun should not put their savings into it if the flat was not in their name. But Varun was firm. He saw no reason for Priyanka to have any insecurity. He went ahead with his father and soon, the flat was purchased in mummyji's name. Priyanka remained in a bad mood and continuously fought with Varun. She even told mummyji about her desire to have the flat in their name. Mummyji was surprised at the way Priyanka was thinking and told her to leave these issues to the males of the house.

Priyanka then, showed her infuriation through other actions. She reduced going in the kitchen on one pretext or another. When mummyji asked her to do any work, she retorted that they should keep a maid as she was getting tired of household chores. She told mummyji bluntly to stop expecting her to be always involved in the kitchen.

During weekdays there was office and during weekends, she had recently joined a kitty party group of the building. They met every week and she wanted to be active in the group. It was a way of getting to know the neighbours. Now that they were going to be permanently settled there, they would need to cultivate good relationships with the neighbours.

Mummyji had not fully recovered from her last illness, even after so many months. She couldn't possibly cope with the entire housework on her own. She had little choice but to agree and soon, there was another maid who came in twice a day to do all the cooking. Priyanka drew pleasure from this change and increased her outings in her social circle, leaving the in-laws to mostly fend for themselves.

To make matters worse, papaji suffered a fall on the stairs one day and fractured his ankle. The doctor told him to be on bed rest for three weeks. Varun was unable to get any leave from office. In fact, he had to go on tour for most of this time.

"Please don't expect me to nurse papaji. I will also not get that many leaves from office," declared Priyanka, making her intentions absolutely clear. At this moment, she forgot how Varun had responded to her father's illness.

Though Varun did not like her attitude, he was left with no option but to keep a male nurse for his father. The nurse was a sincere young man who took good care of his patient and Priyanka continued her routine unhindered. After office, she mingled with the ladies of the building regularly and even started an alumni group of her college friends whom she met frequently.

It was during one such meeting that Anand's name came up. Priyanka felt shivers going down her spine as the last scene with Anand came alive in her mind. It had been so embarrassing. She learnt that Anand was doing well as a bank's probationary officer and had married his girlfriend from college. Priyanka felt wistful, even jealous as she conjectured his happy married life. She forced herself to think about her own situation and vowed to improve it.

❖

On their fourth wedding anniversary, Priyanka persuaded Varun to visit Ambala. She hadn't met her parents for long and she looked forward to this visit. Varun had agreed somewhat reluctantly and hence both found themselves amidst the winter in Ambala on their anniversary.

The fresh, chilly air and the greenery around them lifted their spirits and made them forget their stressful existence in Mumbai. Sanjay and Mamta made their stay as comfortable as they could. Sanjay wanted Shikha to marry at the earliest and urged Priyanka and Varun to find a suitable match for her. Sapna was going to graduate soon.

Mamta raised the issue of extending the family with Priyanka. Priyanka sighed and remembered the incident in Mumbai just a couple of months back. Alka had really pushed the issue of having a grandchild. She often tried to blackmail Varun on this issue by citing their frail health. Varun too was perplexed as to why Priyanka was not conceiving. He even fixed an appointment with a doctor for their check-up but Priyanka refused to go. She bluntly told Varun that she could have a baby only when the home atmosphere was conducive and pleasant. She even hinted that it could be possible only when they had their nuclear family. Varun was too exasperated to hear her viewpoints and would then, shun all such talks. He hoped that better sense would prevail soon.

One fine morning as Priyanka was sneakily taking the contraceptive pill, Varun came in from behind and caught her in the act.

"What medicine are you taking?" He quizzed her. She tried to hide the packet but he took it from her and was shocked to see what it was. A big scene ensued. "You have been deceiving me. It is totally unacceptable and you owe me an explanation." He shouted at her.

"Well, I told you I am not ready for the baby. It is my choice and no one, not even you can force me on this issue." Priyanka firmly answered back.

"You have not been honest with me. That is the bigger point. I am shocked by your actions." Varun screamed before storming out of the house.

It had taken Priyanka days to cajole him back to some normalcy. Varun had not told his parents as he did not want to disturb them further. He hoped that they would not have heard the quarrel. However, he threatened to tell Priyanka's parents if she ever took the pills again. Priyanka wondered what she was going to do. Thus far, she had somehow escaped conceiving but now Varun kept a check that she did not take any pills.

❖

With a sigh, Priyanka came back to the present. Brushing aside her mother's concerns, she told her they were still too young to start a family.

"Rather, you come and stay with us for a while. Shikha and Sapna can manage here," Priyanka implored. Varun kept quiet mostly and didn't join her in this request also. If her parents sensed some friction between Priyanka and Varun, they chose to sensibly remain quiet about it.

After a pleasant stay of a week, it was time to go back for them. The trip was over too soon for Priyanka and she disliked the thought of going back to Mumbai. Upon returning, she tried to kick her blues away by planning a theme based New Year party with her society friends. They decided on a retro theme.

The party was held in the society's club house. The menu and décor was again planned by Priyanka. After the success of her father- in- law's retirement party, she had gained confidence in her skills.

As the music from the 70s and the 80s flowed, everyone got into a dancing mood. Dressed in bell bottoms and a vintage top, Priyanka dragged Varun to the dance floor and for once, they both enjoyed themselves.

As 2020 kicked in, they hugged and kissed, putting all their worries behind.

11

Respa Flu

Every New Year brings with it new promises, new hopes and new dreams; this year was no different for the Chopra household.

Mummyji and papaji hoped they would become grandparents soon, Varun hoped there would be harmony in the house and Priyanka hoped her suffocating misery would end. None of them were prepared however for the avalanche of misfortune that was set to befall, not just them but the entire state of Maharashtra.

The first ominous news broke out at the end of January. There were about thousands of fish being washed ashore dead in a small village in Ratnagiri district. It was an unheard phenomenon. Scientists and researchers started discussing various probable theories about it and news channels were full of surmises.

Before the mystery could be resolved, news about a deadly virus that transmitted from fish to humans started coming in. Many people took ill in Ratnagiri and it became clear that the virus was highly infectious.

Little was known about the new virus except that it attacked the respiratory system and had a high mortality rate. The state government swung into action. Ratnagiri was declared a containment zone and people were advised to not travel there. Still the virus spread like wildfire. The district administration grappled with the increasingly alarming situation and issued advisories on how to avoid the virus. However, the details about the virus were ambiguous. It was not clear what caused it and how it spread. Safe distancing and avoiding crowds were the only preventive ways. It was advised to wear masks if stepping out. Most people did not take these warnings seriously.

In Mumbai, life continued as usual. People lived their lives in the only way they knew – crowded and congested. While the majority dismissed the advisories that predicted a viral outbreak in the entire state, even those who took them seriously had few options. They couldn't sit at home to avoid catching the virus – they had to go out and earn their livelihoods. So they continued to commute in the overcrowded local trains.

The virus started to spread quickly, despite containment measures. Within a month, it had the whole of Mumbai in its grip. The authorities struggled with how to contain the epidemic.

It was something they had not dealt with before. The health department became active. The Disaster Management Act was invoked which had strict restrictions about the movement of people. Still the virus spread unabated and a large number of the populace started to come under its influence. The growing numbers of people affected started to put a strain on the health care system. It was then, that the gravity of the situation started to sink in. The government had to ensure proper health care by making sure that there was no panic. There was a daily bulletin on TV on the latest information about the virus, its spread and the measures being taken to control it.

People began to draw comfort from the benign personality of Chief Medical Officer of AIIMS Mumbai, Dr Randeep Guleria who would often come on these bulletins and share the latest developments. His knowledgeable analysis, easy way of speaking and calm demeanour was reassuring to many troubled minds.

By now, some more details about how the virus attacked the human body had emerged. It attacked the respiratory system and the patients displayed flu-like symptoms. Fever, body-ache and cough were the initial signs. If the virus progressed from the respiratory system and attacked other organs, it could lead to the patient going into coma as multi organ failure struck. The chances of staying alive were minuscule after that. The elderly were thought to be particularly vulnerable to it. There were rumours that the virus was airborne and would sooner or later affect everybody. There was a general panic in the air now and people tried to stay indoors as much as possible.

The TV channels were full of news about the virus and all sorts of statistics around it. The virus was now called RespaFlu. It was estimated that soon, the hospitals and emergency rooms would be overflowing with ill patients and the health care system would be adversely impacted. Stories of numerous doctors and healthcare workers fighting valiantly also started doing the rounds.

❖

Varun switched off the TV after listening to the depressing news of an entire family of four being wiped out due to the virus. He was worried. Both his parents were diabetic and his father also had hypertension. This made their immunity low and the virus could attack them easily. He tried to share his concerns with Priyanka but she was totally indifferent.

"They are just exaggerating, these news channels. Have you seen any case in our neighbourhood? Moreover, it is just like common cold. Swine Flu was much more deadly. This is just a hype created by the pharmaceutical industry and you should know about that! You should ignore all worrying thoughts and stay away from TV," she advised Varun.

But Varun was not convinced. He was thinking of reducing his travel. Being in the pharmaceutical industry, he understood the significance of the virus. He discussed the situation with his colleagues who were equally worried. This was an infectious disease and there was no vaccine for it. No treatment or medicines so prevention was the only cure. The research required for these was already about to commence but that was going to be a time-consuming process.

The scary part was that the source of the virus was unknown. There were multiple theories about it but nothing conclusive had been established yet. It also behaved in an unpredictable manner and attacked different people differently. Some only had a mild fever and cough, some had problems with lungs, some had kidney problems and so on. And some people did not seem to get affected at all. These people were called 'asymptomatic' carriers of the virus as it was not clear whether they could transmit the infection or not.

As the numbers of affected persons grew, the situation became alarming. The entire state was in the hold of virus and soon, the neighbouring states sealed their borders. There could be no travel from Maharashtra to anywhere.

A worried Sanjay called up Priyanka, "Are you all okay, beta? We are so worried from what we saw in the news. I wanted to call you all here but now, the borders are sealed. Just take all precautions." Priyanka assured him they were safe and doing fine. She also promised to call him up daily to update about their well-being.

The administration took one drastic step after another. The most severe was to announce a complete lockdown in the state. A curfew like situation would prevail. The chief minister announced the details on TV and appealed to people to stay indoors. There would be no public transport. The lifeline of Mumbai, the local trains stopped; the shops and the malls were shut down. Even the schools and colleges stopped conducting offline classes. For the first time, the iconic *dabbawalas* of Mumbai stopped operating. There was a ban on any social gathering. Factories and offices could not function.

While the private sector offices quickly switched to the work-from-home system, the government offices that provided essential services were allowed to function with skeletal staff. The poor people were severely hit. As factory after factory shut down, distress arose. Though the government started measures to provide food to the needy, there was no solution for the rising anxiety and panic.

There was a whole process that was prescribed in case anyone felt that he was showing the symptoms. The details had to be given on the government helpline and the testing for the Respaflu was to be done thereafter. In case of positive results, patients had to be kept in designated quarantine centres or hospitals depending on the severity of the case. Government was mulling over the fact if home quarantine could be allowed as hospitals were reaching optimum capacity.

The entire socio-economic spectrum turned chaotic. The tourism sector was among the most badly affected sectors as a result of this epidemic. But hoteliers took the smart move to offer isolation and quarantine facilities in the light of tighter situations in hospitals. Those who could afford or didn't really need strict treatment from hospitals preferred to choose hotel rooms as compared to government hospitals. Most of the hotels started following the sanitisation and isolation centre protocols.

The students were a worried lot. PG set ups and hostels became the epidemic hubs and scared students and bachelors had to bear the brunt of hostile vibes of owners. This left them with no choice but either to move back to their native places or to search for new accommodation even though it was very risky since they might get infected.

Besides, there was another mass scale movement happening. Varun's father was horrified to see on TV the massive lines of migrant labour breaking the lockdown restrictions and walking to reach their native places which were hundreds of miles away from Mumbai. Barefoot children, pregnant women and hungry youth – all united in their urge to reach their hometown or village and leave Maharashtra, carrying their meagre belongings on their heads or slung on their shoulders. Mummyji too was petrified. They had never in their life dreamt that something like this could happen.

❖

For the time being, Varun worked from home but he knew the nature of his job would sooner or later demand visiting the office and making field visits to meet his customers – doctors and dealers. He wondered how he would tackle that. Besides, his company might even venture in the vaccine development programme. That would entail a high level of work for him.

According to reports, the medical fraternity was quite at risk as they selflessly tended to patients and were constantly exposed to the virus. PPE kits, face masks, hand-sanitizers and disinfectant sprays became the new way of life as one stepped out. Varun wondered at the new lingo surrounding them. Community stage spread, lockdown, appropriate behaviour with distancing and mask, immunity, viral load- these words were constantly buzzing around them.

Surprisingly, Priyanka still seemed unaffected by the scary situation. Mummyji wanted everyone to start taking *kadha* to boost up immunity but Priyanka wouldn't do that also. She would keep advising everyone in the house to be normal. Varun was baffled and asked her about it.

"Aren't you afraid? The scene is quite grim yet you go on with your life as if nothing is serious."

"You worry too much," replied Priyanka dismissing his concerns. "See the reports objectively. It is a person-to-person transmission. Young people are not getting seriously affected. The old people just need to stay away from infected persons or wear a face mask. The rest is just an exaggerated hype for commercial benefits."

Varun wondered about how she could be so dismissive about such an alarming situation. His words fell on deaf ears. Rather, Priyanka was getting more affected by the changes in the daily routine. She had to work from her home and there was no going to the office now. Her outings with her friends had stopped. Staying isolated in the house was stifling but she was forced to do so. Varun had decided to even stop going out to get groceries and vegetables. He placed all his orders from the neighbourhood store which delivered them at home or he purchased them online.

❖

Once over dinner, Priyanka didn't miss this opportunity to pass a sarcastic comment.

"I think meat should be totally avoided now as it could be a source of infection," she said, pretending to show concern.

For once mummyji had no answer. But Varun took the discussion forward.

"They say every person could be a potential carrier of the virus. So we also have to ask the maids to stop coming."

Neither mummyji nor Priyanka liked the idea. Mummyji was the first to respond.

"Then who will do all the housework? I can't do everything."

"Look, papa, mummy – you are both in the vulnerable age group," replied Varun. "You have other health issues that make you prone to getting infected. If that happens, it will be a big problem. Already the hospitals are overflowing."

"I think you are making the situation more serious than it actually is," said Priyanka. "Papaji and mummyji are very active. Their blood pressure and sugar level are well under control. Don't scare everyone unnecessarily."

"There will be no discussion on this," Varun said a little aggressively. "The maids will not come from tomorrow. We will all help with the housework by dividing the duties amongst ourselves. As it is, there are no outings now and we have plenty of time."

Priyanka did not like this and countered sharply.

"That is precisely my point. On one hand, there are no outings; on the other hand you want me to suffocate myself in the house with chores. One of our maids live nearby and I don't see why she can't come. As it is now mummyji doesn't do much kitchen work and all the burden is on me. Papaji is firm about his food preferences. And you expect me to cope with it all. And do the sweeping and mopping and washing utensils as well, all day? What about my office work? Should I resign?"

"Why can't...." started Varun angrily, but stopped himself. He suddenly remembered that they had a home loan and EMIs to repay. Without Priyanka's salary, they will not be able to manage expenses.

"In that case, I will do the sweeping and mopping and the utensils. You handle the kitchen. Mummy can do a little dusting when she can," he declared. "But no maids will enter the house."

"You're being impractical," Priyanka grumbled with an angry face. "Let's see how soon you give up." Varun stood his ground.

❖

As two months of lockdown ended, the virus showed no sign of abating. Even in the deserted streets where only fear lurked, it somehow grew in numbers. The lockdown was further extended. By now, Priyanka was tired of household work. She wondered how to get the house help back as Varun was in no mood to compromise on this issue.

She found an answer soon.

One day, somehow their maid managed to come to their house in the wee hours of morning. She stayed very near to their society and hence could reach their place by escaping the checking.

"I am going to my village, didi. Can you give me some money as advance?

You can adjust it against my salary when I come back for work."

"Why are you going? Will you get work in your village?" Priyanka asked.

"No, there is no work in the village. That is why we left our village and came to Mumbai. But there is no work here either. I have to feed my children. Village is less expensive. In the same money, I can last longer in the village, she explained.

"But didi, you are educated. You understand my situation. Please allow me to come and work for you. I will come early morning and exercise all precautions. Whatever you say, I will do. Please, for my children's sake," she said and almost sobbed.

"Let me see. I will speak to mummyji. Come back tomorrow morning and I will let you know."

"God bless you, didi," said the overwhelmed maid. At least there was one person who was willing to help her. Others did not even try.

The crisis was bringing out different facets of human psychology. On one hand, there were committed doctors who, like warriors, went on their path of duty fearlessly and on the other hand, self-centeredness was rising among people in general. While there were NGOs and even religious organizations which were distributing food, there were also people who were hoarding food stuff, dismissing labour from factories and workers from offices without any compassion. Even black-marketing of life-saving drugs had started.

Priyanka was not troubled by these bitter realities. Her sole issue was that she was tired of doing the household work and seized this opportunity to try to get Varun to change his mind.

"We must not be selfish but rather we should help out the maid," she told him. "She has been with us for so long. I will make sure that mummyji does not interact with her. I will supervise her myself." But Varun did not budge.

"Never!" he said. "There will be no maid in this house. I won't take a chance with my parents' lives."

❖

When the maid came the next day, Priyanka gave her one thousand rupees – not enough to buy tickets to go to her village, but enough to survive for a few days.

"Wait for a few days. Don't go to your village now. I am sure I will convince Varun soon. I will call on your mobile as soon as I have any news."

The maid was only too happy to stay on. There was nothing for her in the village – just a life of exploitation and no future for her children. She would only go there if she was absolutely desperate and had no other option.

Priyanka wondered how she could get Varun to change his mind. Then she smiled as she thought of how she had twisted her ankle when she was trying to woo Anand in college. The next morning, while she was bathing, Priyanka slipped in the bathroom and sprained her wrist. The bathroom's floor had become slippery because of lack of proper cleaning and she promptly blamed Varun for her fall. After all, he had said that cleaning would be his responsibility.

When Varun saw her, her wrist was all blue and she was trying to tie a crepe bandage around it. He immediately examined it and while no bones appeared to have been broken, it was totally swollen.

"Gosh, it is hurting so much," moaned Priyanka. "Should I show it to the doctor?" The predicament was that going to any clinic was risky as one could easily catch the infection from there. So she had to make do with a crepe bandage and painkillers. But she made it clear that she couldn't do any household chores in her present condition.

"I will manage," mummyji said valiantly. "It's only a question of a few days."

But Varun knew that was not an option. Mummy couldn't manage everything, no matter how much she tried. He didn't want her to fall ill with overwork. Handling papa too at this time was itself a full-time job. And he could only help in a limited manner. So left with no choice, he asked Priyanka to call the maid.

He told his parents to stay away from the maid and not interact with her at all. During the time she was in the house, they should stay in their room. He also asked Priyanka to ensure that the maid washed her hands carefully and wore a mask all the time. These two precautions were essential in avoiding the infection. Priyanka was only too happy to concur.

The maid started coming twice a day and Priyanka heaved a sigh of relief. She made sure not to remove the crepe bandage for two weeks and by then, Varun had become accustomed to the maid working in the house.

12

A Bleak Scenario

A few days later, Varun received a call from his boss. He was required to travel to Pune for a few days for urgent work related to the vaccination research programme. It appeared that there was some initial success about isolating the DNA of the virus and the company wanted to project it carefully. His company had arranged a special pass for him to travel. He would stay in the company guest house at Pune. Varun knew he couldn't avoid it. It was fortunate that the maid was there, otherwise it would have been impossible to manage the house in his absence. But he was scared of leaving the house.

"I don't know what to do," he told Priyanka. "I can't refuse to go. But the circumstances are so risky. Pune's situation is more serious than Mumbai's situation."

"I think you worry too much needlessly," replied Priyanka brusquely. "Everything is being exaggerated excessively. And young people like us are not at risk. Even if we catch the virus, it will be like a mild flu, which will go away in a few days. You shouldn't fret but focus on your job."

Varun felt strangely reassured and wished he was as confident as Priyanka was. He started packing and realized he would be leaving home after nearly three months.

When Varun left for Pune, Priyanka felt more bored. It was fine during the day because of the office. But in the evening and night, she felt lonely. She decided to start taking walks in the society compound. She brushed aside the fears of her in-laws and told them that by now it was evident that the virus was not airborne. She wanted to resume her routine of meeting friends but most of them were too scared to do so or venture out. So for the time being, she had to be content with solitary walks.

When Varun came back, he had to be in home isolation for a week as per rules. This upset Priyanka even more as she had to move out of the room and could not even watch TV. Annoyed, she would spend time in the evenings either talking to her parents – who were very worried for them – or she would talk to her friends.

Soon Priyanka started going out to buy vegetables and fruits. Varun wasn't very comfortable about this but then, Priyanka had her arguments ready.

"These online vendors are just giving cold storage vegetables and fruits. They are expensive and not at all healthy. We need to build immunity at this time. The places I visit are following social distancing. I wear a mask all the time,' Priyanka assured Varun.

Varun shrugged and let her be since he knew that Priyanka wouldn't really understand her concern. However, he felt uneasy. There was no cure from the virus in sight. Nor was a vaccine present in the near future. Varun now knew that the vaccine would take a year to be available in the market. They needed a miracle much before that. Despite all containment measures, the virus had spread to the interiors of the state now. What was more worrisome was that the strain was beginning to mutate and become more severe. The death statistics were alarming. The positivity rate was still on the rise which meant that the disease was spreading fast. The recoveries were also there but the air of panic and gloom was thicker. Neighbouring states were on guard. Parallels were drawn to the Spanish flu outbreak almost a thousand years ago. It was strange that even after so much time, medical science could only offer the same trilogy of social distance, masks and hand washing as the way to deal with the epidemic. People looked at old predictions and said doomsday was near. All in all, it was a bleak scenario.

Varun yearned for normalcy and he was not alone. Papa and mummy stayed huddled in their room most of the time and they had become quiet and withdrawn. Varun would often go and spend time with them but there was an air of desolation which he could not mitigate. He prayed for their good health and hoped they all survived this phase of life.

13

Helpless Prisoners

The lockdown was extended for another month. There was a sense of gloom in the air. The fear factor was high. The economy of the state was badly affected. The government had already sought financial help from the central government. Other state governments also offered medical and financial aid. The Indian Council of Medical Research was involved in developing a vaccine.

Varun's company was hopeful of starting trials for the vaccine soon but it was a long drawn process. Even the World Health Organization was alerted to the situation. The fact of the matter was that the economic capital of India was facing a shut down.

Amid all these problems, Priyanka informed Varun that the maid had called. She had to rush to her village due to the death of her relative. She was expected to be away for two weeks. "We will have to manage somehow in her absence," Priyanka concluded with a frown on her face.

Varun wasn't too perturbed. He offered to go back to the old schedule they followed earlier. "I would do the cleaning and wash utensils happily, I will even cook for you," he said in an attempt to cheer up Priyanka.

Priyanka was only too glad to take up his offer. Mummyji cribbed a little on seeing Varun too much in the kitchen but he pacified her somehow.

Then, Varun's company wanted him to go to Pune again. There were further developments for the vaccination programme and it appeared trials could begin shortly. While Varun thought that was good news, he knew he would have to be away for at least a week. Just before he was to leave, Priyanka developed a sore throat with mild cold. But there was no fever. Varun got worried, but Priyanka was still unperturbed.

"I think I should postpone the trip," Varun said. 'I can't be away for so long when you are not well. And the maid is also not there."

"Relax, Varun. It's nothing. Just a seasonal sore throat. I always get it at this time of the year. All your travel arrangements are already made. The curfew pass is in your name. If you postpone your trip just for a sore throat and cold, what will your seniors think? Don't make a fool of yourself and go for your tour.

"How will you manage without the maid? And what if you get a fever, Priyanka?"

"Don't worry. The world won't come to an end if the sweeping and mopping is not done every day. I will manage. Don't worry. This tour may turn out to be very important for your career, you must go," she emphasized.

Varun felt happy when he observed this change in Priyanka. For the first time after marriage, she had, on her own, volunteered to accept responsibility. It was good to see that she cared for his career, not for her personal comfort. But he wasn't totally convinced if she could manage on her own. He also hoped fervently that her ill-health was just seasonal allergy and nothing more. Very reluctantly, he left for his trip.

He was worried enough to call Priyanka several times a day during the entire trip. Each time, Priyanka told him everything was well.

❖

When he came back, Priyanka seemed fine. She said that she had mild fever for a couple of days, but it was gone now. So was the cough. She did feel tired sometimes, but that was because she had to work extra. She took three days leave from office to be able to cope with the situation.

"But why didn't you tell me all this when I called from Pune?" protested Varun.

"There was no point getting you worried," Priyanka replied. "What could you do from there?"

"I could have rushed back."

"For what? See everything is all right now."

Varun had no answer to that. Perhaps he was worrying too much, unnecessarily. Anyway, he would be at home now to oversee everything – he was supposed to be in self-isolation for a week after coming back from Pune. He had worked hard to develop the marketing strategy during the tour. He was now feeling a little tired and the forced rest was indeed welcome.

❖

But everything was not alright. After three days, both mummyji and papaji woke up with sore throats and fever. Varun knew intuitively that the virus had struck them. He trembled to think about how he would handle it all. He asked them both to be confined to their room and use the masks. As per the laid down procedure, he notified the government authorities who came in a couple of hours and took the samples of his parents. Mummyji and papaji felt nervous but were hardly able to speak due to the rising cough. They were all advised home isolation till the results came.

Priyanka, for once, was quiet and also felt a little apprehensive when she saw that the lab staff in PPE kits had arrived to take samples.

The test results came the next day. Both were positive. Varun's worst nightmare had come true. He didn't know what to do next. Both mummy and papa had a terrible cough and even breathlessness. The health authorities advised immediate hospitalization, looking at their existing health issues. The house was marked as being under quarantine. Varun and Priyanka were told to not leave the house and follow all precautions. Varun could sense the fear in his neighbours as the building's WhatsApp group spread the news to everyone.

An ambulance came and took mummy and papa to the designated hospital for treatment. Varun had tears in his eyes as he saw his parents being taken away – almost like helpless prisoners. He wanted to accompany the ambulance till the hospital at least, but it was pointless as visitors were not allowed inside the hospital. Moreover, he himself was under quarantine.

There was a shortage of testing kits hence the authorities were only testing people who had clear symptoms. So the doctor told him and Priyanka to be alert and watch out for any symptoms. Until then, they should remain in strict isolation at home for two weeks. They suspected Varun may have picked up the virus during his Pune trip and asked him to inform his office to put everyone he had met under isolation as well. He was also supposed to inform the staff at the company guest house where he had stayed to do the same. Contact tracing was indeed the norm of the day.

But Varun's thought process was on a different track. He asked Priyanka about the details of her illness once more. Priyanka understood where this was leading. She tried to dismiss Varun's questioning.

"Varun, let's focus on the present. Both mummyji and papaji need to recover. Let us pray for that."

"I need to know why you didn't inform me about your illness and why you took it so casually. You have been going out and also interacting with the maid. Supposing you had a mild case of Respa Flu and then, you passed it on to papa and mummy," Varun said out his thoughts aloud.

Priyanka was aghast but for a change, she kept quiet. This could snowball, she thought and again advised Varun to not think like this.

Varun could not visit the hospital as he himself was in isolation. He contacted the hospital and spoke to the treating doctor. He was informed that both Jagat and Alka were showing fluctuating oxygen levels. They had been put on oxygen support. The main aim was to prevent lung damage. If need be, a CT-scan would be done. The doctor told him they were doing their best and he would have to be patient. Varun was filled with immense gratitude for the doctor fraternity. He could only imagine what they were going through.

Deep down, Varun still wondered how his parents caught the deadly virus and could only think of Priyanka being the cause. He felt disdain towards her and struggled to contain his thoughts.

❖

Three days passed, but there was no improvement in their state. Their temperature continued to be over 101. Varun asked one of his friends Chand to visit the hospital and get the correct status. His friend was allowed only till the waiting area, which was teeming with worried relatives. The duty nurse told him that there was no improvement in their health as of now.

Apart from the oxygen saturation, other parameters were more or less stable. Later, Chand described to Varun how sometimes, the sound of wrecking cough and even moaning escaped outside and further increased the prevailing dejection. Varun requested his boss to try and get him in touch with Dr Randeep Guleria, so that he could see papa and mummy and give an opinion about the line of treatment. His boss had some contacts in the health ministry and he promised to help.

Since Varun couldn't go to the hospital himself, he regularly tried to contact the duty doctor for updates. On day fourth, the helpful duty nurse made him speak to his mother but the signal was weak and mummy couldn't hear anything. They could just hear her crying. This upset Varun even more and throwing all caution to the wind, he made himself a large drink. He soon grew aggressive. Priyanka had never seen him like this. She tried to keep out of his way but Varun followed her wherever she went.

"I need to know what happened when I was away. If you had fever, why didn't you isolate yourself? Didn't you think it could be RespaFlu and that you could infect papa and mummy?" He said vehemently. "Varun, please calm down, don't think so negatively. I thought the fever was due to seasonal change and the allergy which I always get."

"No!" Varun stomped his fit angrily on the coffee table. "You have never really cared for them. You are just a self-centred person. You know what, sometimes I feel we should end our marriage." Priyanka was stunned as she heard Varun blurt out his inner feelings. She kept trying to pacify him but Varun was not in his senses. "Yes, divorce is the only solution" he kept mumbling in his drunken stupor before finally sleeping off.

❖

Sleep eluded Priyanka though. She thought about the entire chain of events and felt suddenly scared.

What if I had indeed passed on the infection to mummyji and papaji?

She had definitely been negligent and casual in her approach. More demonic thoughts possessed her as she tossed and turned in the night. She thought of all her altercations with mummyji. She started to realize in her heart that she was also responsible for the messy situation at her home. She had not thought of them as her own parents and had almost always put her interests first. And then a bigger question began to haunt her.

Did I want this to happen? When the whole world was exercising precaution, why had I been so careless in inviting exposure? What had I been thinking?

She was tormented by her questions but there were no answers. She was also shocked at Varun's strong expression of divorce.

Did he really mean it? What would I do without him?

In fact she could not visualize a life without papaji and mummyji either. Now that they were not there, she missed their presence in the house. Many times she felt that mummyji was in her own room and was going to come out and chide her for something. Worked up, she just prayed for their recovery and fell into an uneasy sleep.

❖

In the morning Varun was still sour and did not speak to her properly.

"Look Varun, I am sorry," Priyanka tried to apologize.

"Sorry for what? You just don't realize how much unhappiness you have brought to my parents. Look at their state now. Now please do your work and let me focus on getting an appointment of Dr Guleria." Varun was curt and ignored her for the rest of the day.

The duty nurse informed that there was no progress in their health. Rather papaji was having difficulty in breathing even with oxygen support, and doctors were contemplating if a ventilator was needed. This made Varun more restless. The day passed somehow. He didn't drink that night but neither could he talk to Priyanka. An uneasy silence lay between them. The crisis, instead of bringing them closer, was driving them apart.

14

A Wave of Change

As the attendant summoned them inside the court-room, Varun scrambled up to his feet and looked around for Priyanka. He displayed a profound contempt when he spotted her, calmly entering the courtroom. His lawyer nudged him to greet the judge as he entered the courtroom and Varun complied with his instructions.

The family court at Bandra, was an impersonal building, housing small chambers of judges. The usual hustle-bustle of courts was replaced by a tense environment here. As families were either saved or destroyed, individuals walking in the narrow corridors wore either ebullient or anguished expressions. The courtrooms too, were devoid of any histrionics as normally depicted in movies, but were rather painted with silence and sometimes tears.

The judge took his chair and looked sombrely at both of them. Varun's lawyer briefed him about the counselling process done so far. He explained that Varun was the one who had sent the divorce notice to Priyanka citing incompatible differences. Priyanka was resisting the divorce and was fighting her case. She had pleaded that there was no such issue between them and the divorce should not be granted.

A perplexed look came upon the judge as he heard the details. Though used to hearing varied causes for divorce, it was rare that a case like this came up. Intrigued, he turned to Varun and asked,

"Can you elaborate on what are the differences that are propelling you to end all ties with this lady?"

Varun kept silent. His lawyer again nudged him to speak up as the judge was known to have a reputation for being impatient. Varun spoke in a low tone," Your honour, I do not have much to say. I feel a compulsive need to be away from her and a divorce is the only way out."

"Is either of you having an affair?" the judge asked. Varun replied in the negative. But he grew increasingly fidgety. The judge then turned to Priyanka and asked her to explain her side of things.

Priyanka spoke softly but firmly, "We have been married for five years. It was an arranged marriage and I have adapted to the demands of a joint family. I am not really able to understand why Varun is doing this. I have asked him umpteen times, since he has filed for divorce but each time I draw a blank. Varun and this marriage are very important to me. Even my parents think so. I do not want this divorce and plead with your honour to dismiss the case."

Varun grew agitated on hearing this and gulped down a glass of water. He looked at the lawyer who took the cue and started speaking on behalf of Varun.

"My lord, my client is willing to give her alimony as per his means.There are no children involved. It can be an open and shut case. Already six months have passed in counselling and my client is on the brink of depression. I plead with your honour to grant the divorce so that my client can move on in life."

"No, your honour," Priyanka said in a raised voice. "There are no grounds for any such decision. I am happy with Varun and will even try more to keep him happy. He is perhaps disturbed by his parents' sudden demise and is acting in an unstable way of mind since then…"

"Stop, just stop, "Varun almost screamed, his face all flushed. "Don't mention my parents! You have no right to do so. You made their life miserable," Varun stopped abruptly and glared at Priyanka. She kept quiet but glared back at Varun and the judge was quick to sense the animosity, now permeating the atmosphere.

Priyanka spoke again, this time with a tinge of intensity, "My lord! Trust me, there was no such issue. We had some differences of opinion but which couple doesn't have them? And Varun is just magnifying the whole thing because as I said, he is disturbed. His parents have left us. My parents live in a distant city and now, instead of this drama, Varun should focus on starting a family with me."

"Drama, you call this a drama?" Varun again cried out. "You never cared for them, you wanted us to live separately and then, when you saw you were not succeeding, you killed them. Yes, you murdered them!"

❖

Priyanka awoke with a startle as the words from her dream still echoed in her ears. She wiped the sweat on her forehead and gulped down some water. She then checked the phone to see if there was any update from the hospital. When she saw no fresh message, she tried to relax and took deep breaths. Her dream had shaken her.

Varun was sleeping peacefully and suddenly Priyanka felt like crying. She thought of the alienation that she had felt in the early days of marriage. It was difficult to pinpoint the source of this unsettling feeling – perhaps, it was the ruckus caused by the uncle in the wedding, the spurning of gifts they had lovingly bought from Hong Kong and finally mummyji's stern admonishment to her over her clothes that had sowed the seeds of discord. Things had only worsened from there. They had not been able to come together as a family. On her part, she too had started putting her happiness first. She realised that she had been obstinate at times when she could have been more accommodative. She had even deceived Varun as she did not want to conceive.

She felt a deep feeling of repentance. Her stubbornness and myopic thinking had made her behave abhorrently. Her mind went back to the many tussles and arguments. She thought of the constant friction on the multiple issues and it all appeared frivolous now as the grim reality of life and death struck her. She thought of her parents and how they had brought her up- it was surely not for being disrespectful and cantankerous. She realized how patient Varun had been with her. He deserved much more than what he had got.

Out of nowhere, thoughts of Anand also came to her she recalled her dejection and then, her joy in marrying Varun.

Where had all my happiness gone in all these years? She thought as she finally got up to start her day. Her mind kept churning throughout the day.

Her thoughts again went back to the early days of marriage as she tried desperately to recall the point from where the problems had started. She remembered again how she had felt estranged because of the various disharmonious incidents and then, how her rebellious nature had led her to behave in the impetuous manner. Alienation suddenly made her think of Sapna. Had she, along with Shikha, not alienated her totally from their lives? They were her only family and yet, both of them had not shown any kindness to her. And the shy girl had never reacted. She had always been in their shadow but had never complained to dad or ma.

Priyanka's heart went out to her as she realized how the demure Sapna had endured the hostility meted out to her. On an impulse, she called her up.

"Didi, how are you? Is all well?" said a surprised Sapna, on hearing her voice. "Yes, everything is now fine," said Priyanka to a bewildered Sapna.

"I just want to say that Shikha and I are there for you. Never feel alone in life. While we can't bring back chachu and chachi, we are there for you."

Priyanka grew emotional as she voiced her thoughts. Sapna understood that some upheaval had happened in her elder cousin's life.

She replied with all her poise, "Didi, I have never felt otherwise. Yes, I was distraught and even afraid when they passed away but I knew I had to accept my situation. And yes, sometimes I felt that you and Shikha didi did not want me in your home, but I always believed that in relationships, sometimes you win and sometimes you lose. Tauji and taiji gave me so much love that it compensated for a lot. And I was grateful for a wholesome family life again. That is why I tried to never complain but give you the respect that you deserved." Priyanka was astounded to hear such wise words from the young girl.

If she could be grateful in life and accept her situation, Priyanka definitely had a lot more to be thankful for. She reassured Sapna of her love and slowly disconnected the phone, thinking she must have a talk with Shikha too on this issue. They must now make amends and treat her as their own from now on.

Unaware of what was going on inside Priyanka's mind, Varun continued to cold shoulder her. He just somehow wanted to visit the hospital and see his parents. He also was occupied with arranging the visit of Dr Guleria.

He was too consumed by these thoughts to notice that there was a difference in Priyanka's attitude. As she gained insights about her behaviour, she felt a wave of change rising in her. She knew that she had to set things right. She now wanted to amend her flaws and build a happy home. She wanted mummyji and papaji to recover and be at home. A home which she would adorn with love and care. She just hoped it was not too late.

Will I be able to do it alone? In a family, everyone should accept each other. But will I be accepted as one of them and ever get a perfect family life?

Filled with these thoughts, she had withdrawn into herself and yet her actions were speaking of her change. She started praying. She replaced her earlier indifference with care and concern towards her in-laws. She made it a point to keep their room clean regularly and kept a track of hospital updates. Her mind was still in turmoil but she knew that these steps taken by her would go a long way in cementing her relationships.

❖

On the sixth day of hospitalization, Varun got the news that Dr Guleria would be visiting the hospital as a special case and would examine some patients. Varun swung into action. He got his boss to reach out to Dr Guleria and he kindly agreed to see his parents. Varun was tense the whole day till he got a call from hospital in the evening. Dr Guleria had changed medications and had expressed confidence that both would recover soon. He had advised against the use of ventilator at this point of time. His visit had a positive impact on everyone. Varun also relaxed.

That night Priyanka had a vivid dream again. She saw herself in a pool, desperately trying to swim. She knew she had to save herself from drowning and she threw her arms and legs around in desperation. Then suddenly, a coach called out to her from the side and told her to calm down. He guided her towards the bars and she held onto them for dear life.

While she continued to breathe heavily, she realized she had almost swum by herself to safety. She looked around for the coach to thank him but he had disappeared. Priyanka pondered over her dream in the morning. She didn't know swimming and wondered from where the whole idea had crept in her mind. Out of curiosity, she researched and found out what such a dream meant; there was a satisfying smile on her face.

'If you dream you are learning to swim, it means the time has come to make a change or to start over.' According to Google, 'this dream should be encouraging, promising and should give you hope. You can make things right again, in a completely new setting, but it is going to be tough.' Priyanka absorbed it all in. She was on the right path. Her resolve to have new beginnings further strengthened.

In the next two days, even the oxygen saturation of papaji and mummyji started to improve. The news cheered up both Varun and Priyanka. To celebrate, Priyanka thought of cooking something special. She cooked Varun's favourite biryani and raita. As they both started to eat dinner, she held Varun's hand and said softly.

"I am sorry, Varun. I realize I have acted unreasonably in all these years. Somehow, I could not accept mummyji's way of life. Perhaps I was immature. I felt that they have also not accepted me. But I can see now that she only wanted us to be a harmonious unit."

Tears started flowing as she continued to speak. "Their illness and the way you responded have compelled me to introspect. It has made me realize a lot of things. I need to alter my attitude and perspectives and become more accepting of them. They will surely reciprocate. You may not have felt it but I have already changed a lot. Just as I want long life and good health for my parents, the same is the case with you. And trust me, I want the same now."

Varun stopped eating as he could not believe what Priyanka was saying. He knew he had been nasty to her in the past few days, but he actually thought her to be the source of his parents's illness. He still did not know how to remove that doubt. Priyanka continued to express remorse about her mistakes.

Varun stopped her and told her to relax. Beyond that, he could not say anything. He also thought her change might be temporary and soon, the hostile atmosphere in the house would be back. Priyanka sensed his thoughts.

"Time is the best healer," she told him philosophically and went on quietly about her dinner. As she ate, she thought about the latest test she had heard about. It showed if the person had developed antibodies as an immune response to the virus. People who had been infected by it, normally had a positive result. An idea came to her. She cleared up the dining table and the kitchen and slept with her thoughts.

In the morning, as Varun called up the hospital, she said, "I have already spoken to the duty doctor. They are doing better, it seems the worst is over and the fever is also much less now. After Dr Guleria's visit, the response from the hospital is much more elaborate." Varun almost hugged her upon hearing this.

"I also wanted to say," she continued, "I want to go for the antibody test. I do not want you to have any doubt that I caused mummyji and papaji to fall ill. Otherwise it will always weigh on your mind and affect our relationship."

Varun thought before speaking, "I agree. This doubt needs to go. You have come up with a good idea but what if…" he didn't finish his sentence.

"Well, we can always go for a divorce if your fears come true," Priyanka said soberly as she started to lay down the breakfast. Varun kept quiet but he knew he had to know the source of the virus; otherwise it would continue to gnaw at him. This test seemed the only way out. They decided to get the test done for both as soon as it was possible.

Meanwhile, the viral load reduced drastically for both Jagat and Alka and they started breathing easily. The oxygen levels became stable and the cough was almost gone. The doctor opined they could go home as soon as they tested negative, which would take another week. Varun and Priyanka's quarantine would end at the same time.

❖

Varun had arranged for the antibody test for them to be done from their home. The sample was duly collected and the report would come the next day, the technician informed. It was a tense night for them before the results came.

Priyanka could hardly sleep and though she had a long chat with Shikha in the night, she refrained from telling her any details. Varun too was full of thoughts. He could sense there was a change in Priyanka but what if she indeed had been the source of the infection for his parents.

Will I be able to forgive her? He hoped it would not come to that.

Priyanka felt tears glistening in her eyes as she saw the report that came in the morning. She had been tested negative and so had Varun. She was not the cause. She felt relief surging through her and she almost sobbed. She realized that she was fortunate to have escaped the wrath of the virus. And now she had been given the gift of a second chance to salvage her home. Never again would she behave the way she did. Her self-centredness had already been replaced by selflessness.

As Varun saw the report, relief washed over him too. His doubts had been laid to rest. "I am sorry," Varun said softly and after long, held her closely in a warm embrace. "It's me who needs to apologise, I was indeed careless. But god has been kind."

Priyanka replied. The maid must have been the asymptomatic carrier; Varun concluded and forbade her from thinking about this issue any further. He continued to caress her and they made passionate love after long.

❖

Jagat and Alka recovered steadily. They tested negative and soon, it was home-coming day for them. Varun eagerly went to the hospital to bring them home. They had grown feeble and were waiting desperately to go back to the comfort zone of their home. All of them had tears in their eyes as they saw each other. A battle had indeed been won.

During the way back home, they told Varun about the despair they had encountered in the hospital and had almost given up at a point in time. Dr Guleria's visit had been the turning point. They thanked him profusely. In fact, they were grateful to all the treating doctors and nursing staff who were handling this deadly epidemic with courage, putting duty before self.

Varun did not share any details about what had transpired between Priyanka and him, nor did he inform them about the change in Priyanka, as he wanted them to discover it for themselves.

15

Precious Petals

An ebullient Priyanka welcomed them with the traditional aarti. As she bent down to touch their feet, she had tears in her eyes. "Welcome home," she tried to smile as she said it. She felt a huge relief that mummyji and papaji were back home. She knew that she would now take utmost care of them and give them no room for complaints. She had decorated their room with flowers and hand–made banners.

Both mummyji and papaji were surprised at her efforts but they were still feeling drained and overwhelmed. The past few days had been nothing short of a nightmare for everyone. Having seen death from close quarters, Alka and Jagat were still shaky and just wanted to stay as calm as possible.

"Lunch is ready," Priyanka announced. They all assembled at the dinner table. A light but delicious meal awaited them and Alka enjoyed her favourite khichdi, served steaming hot by Priyanka.

"Please take proper rest and lots of fluids. Coconut water is a must. And also remember to take the medicines in time," Varun told them.

"Don't worry! I'm there at home only now. I will remind mummyji and papaji. In fact, I've even ordered medicine organizer sets for them, so that everything is systematically kept." Priyanka said as she started to clear the table. Alka and Jagat continued to feel surprised at Priyanka's new, caring behaviour but chose to not comment on it. They were still worried about the state of their health. They had to recuperate fully. The virus had earned a dubious reputation of causing post-recovery complications. Staying indoors was the only option for them as of now. They did not want the maid to come in as they were sure she had been the source of infection. But they also wanted to avoid a conflict with Priyanka on this issue. They knew Priyanka could be rigid on such matters.

Silently, they retreated into their room for a nap but soon, Alka heard noises from the kitchen. She got up to see the cause and found Priyanka doing the dishes. "The maid will come and do it. Why are you doing it?" she asked.

"Oh mummyji we forgot to tell you. We removed the maid. She was possibly the source of infection to you and papaji . It's better to not call her till the situation improves." Priyanka said politely.

"But, I won't be able to do much in the kitchen now. How will you manage alone?" Alka wondered out loud.

"Mummyji please don't embarrass me. It is my duty to handle it all. I have formed a good schedule wherein I do the household chores before and after my office hours. After all, the commuting time is saved and I am less tired too. Besides, you are just back home from hospital after such a severe illness. You must not even think of household chores. Please leave it to me. I will certainly take your advice as and when I need it on cooking matters. Varun also helps me. It is a great blessing of god that we all are together again. So please let us enjoy that," Priyanka spoke with such earnestness that now Alka was intrigued. She could not believe that her errant daughter–in–law was showing so much concern for her. Puzzled, she went back to her room and whispered to Jagat about the change in Priyanka.

"Well, it is a good thing, if it is so. Maybe it is superficial and temporary, so take things in your stride and don't overthink," Jagat said pragmatically.

❖

Over the next few days, Jagat also was forced to think about the change of heart in Priyanka. She worked tirelessly, doing the cooking and cleaning expertly in the morning. She then did her office work from 10 a.m. with a small lunch break at 1.30 wherein she checked on both of them. She was free at 6 p.m.

and after relaxing with a cup of tea that Varun invariably made, she entered the kitchen and made dinner. Varun's working hours were flexible and he gladly helped Priyanka as much as he could. She enjoyed this companionship. Her cooking skills had improved considerably, not just because of YouTube recipes and tips from Mamta but because she had now added the most important ingredient in it –love.

The hospital stay had impacted mummyji and papaji in many ways. Lying helpless on the hospital beds, both had reflected about life, death and relationships. While Jagat thought how Varun would cope in case anything happened to them, Alka strangely had thoughts about Priyanka. She had felt that perhaps, she had been harsh with Priyanka. She had expected her to adhere to all norms that had been followed by her unquestioningly, but she had forgotten times had changed. Moreover, she had not really let go of Varun and had wanted to exercise all control over him.

She should have given more space to her newlywed son. She also thought that she had not truly treated Priyanka as a daughter. Priyanka was impetuous, no doubt, but as an elder she could have hand-holded her more gently into the ways of her home. She had perhaps wanted her authority to prevail in the house and perceived Priyanka as a threat to that. These fleeting thoughts resurfaced now as she saw Priyanka transformed into quite an ideal daughter-in-law.

While she could not fathom the reasons for her change, mummyji nonetheless vowed to herself that she would support

Priyanka more. As it is, life was uncertain and tranquillity in relationships was very important. She expressed her views and happiness to Varun, who also revelled in the harmony that prevailed in their house. It was a pleasant environment now. He could never have thought that the virus would leave such a positive aftermath for him. The precious petals of his life, which were falling earlier, were now woven in a fragrant garland.

"All of us are loving your new version," he told Priyanka as she got ready to sleep. "In fact, I sense a change in everyone. There is better understanding among all of us. It is as if pieces of a jigsaw puzzle, which were flying here and there till now, have suddenly fallen into place. Things are much more pleasant when there is no bickering on any issue. I am amazed at the composure with which you deal with everything now. Truly, how has so much turnaround happened? At least share with me," he urged Priyanka, who smiled in return.

"The vamp in me has left me," was all she replied naughtily.

❖

The next week it was Alka and Jagat's wedding anniversary. They could not go out to celebrate so Priyanka thought of making it a special day at home itself. She ordered a grey- golden Banarasi sari for Alka and a colour co-ordinated kurta set for Jagat. She planned an elaborate menu for the dinner. She also arranged flower garlands through an online app and painstakingly compiled an audio-visual presentation from the old photo albums.

Alka and Jagat gracefully accepted the gifts and wore them in the evening. The high point was the joint cooking of chicken by both Varun and Priyanka. Jagat told Priyanka she needn't go out of her way to cook it but Priyanka insisted. Varun ordered meat online and further cleaned it up. Priyanka made the gravy and together, they churned out the most delicious butter chicken ever.

"I am so happy Varun has not gone on his father," mummyji said. "It's so good that Varun helps Priyanka in the kitchen. You must learn something from him," she jokingly chided Jagat. Priyanka felt a wave of joy run through her upon hearing this. Truly, change begets change. Then, they had a family video call with all near and dear ones joining in. Sanjay, Mamta, Shikha and Sapna were delighted to see and greet them, as was mausiji.

"We are at a loss of words. May god bless both of you and shower all happiness on you," an emotional Jagat said to them after the call was over. The day had been made memorable by Priyanka's meticulous planning and execution.

❖

The next morning, Priyanka woke up feeling nauseous. She thought it was food poisoning but then, something struck her. She immediately called up her chemist and soon, the good news was confirmed. She wondered about when she could have conceived but could not pin point it. She was also not too sure of her reaction but looking at the excitement around her, she told herself to stop thinking.

Mummyji and papaji were exuberant. Varun was ecstatic. Alka mentally went over the special recipes she knew for expecting mothers. She also voiced her concerns about Priyanka's workload. She told her to reduce it.

"Varun will help me in the evening and we will manage. Even your papaji should do his share now. You need to take it easy," she told her daughter-in-law. Priyanka enjoyed the care and attention. She started visualising about the baby.

Motherhood would definitely be a very different experience. She thought. It entailed responsibility and with Varun, she felt ready for it. Her parents were equally happy and she wished she could meet them soon.

The bliss was short lived. Two weeks later, as Priyanka came out of the bathroom, she slipped and fell badly on the floor. Somehow she got up and reached her bed. She called out to mummyji and by the time she reached, Priyanka was having severe pain and cramps. Scared, she wanted to think no further. Papaji told them to go the hospital immediately. Varun arranged an ambulance and they rushed to the nearby hospital. But the miscarriage could not be prevented.

Priyanka sobbed the whole day. Alka stroked her head and told her to accept god's will but, it offered no solace to Priyanka. Jagat was quiet. Varun was shocked and withdrawn as well. He also felt guilty as he felt it was his fault that the bathroom floor was not cleaned well. But it was Priyanka who was most affected. A deep sense of loss permeated her and she alternated between tears and introspection. She thought of her desire to not have a child earlier.

Was this a karmic consequence then? She thought of her earlier falls of similar nature and shuddered as she was reminded of her thinking at that time.

Was I facing this trauma now because of my earlier actions? But had I not realized my mistakes and tried to atone for them?

Her mind continuously buzzed with these thoughts. She could not confide even to Varun. She fell into depression. She could not get rid of her negative thoughts and became a pale, gloomy shadow of who she was. She would barely eat and became weak.

Alka was worried and revealed her concern to Mamta. Both of them discussed as to how to bring Priyanka out of this shell. Travel was difficult, if not improbable. But Varun wanted either Shikha or Sapna to visit them. He himself was feeling so shattered that he was hardly able to console his wife. There was a system of getting travel pass issued on valid grounds. He spoke to the authorities and cited medical reasons for getting a travel pass issued. It was decided that as Shikha had exams coming up, Sapna would come and spend some time with Priyanka.

The shy Sapna had blossomed over the years in a sensible and mature girl. Though she still spoke less, everyone could see that her heart was in the right place. She had learnt excellent housekeeping skills from Mamta and as soon as she arrived in the Chopra household, she took over the kitchen with ease.

'Beta, you are a godsend. Besides handling the chores, it is your graceful attitude which is a blessing," Alka appreciated her. Priyanka too welcomed her but refrained from speaking much. Varun decided to let both of them bond together and quietly shifted to the living room.

At night, after feeding Priyanka with a light daliya, Sapna settled in besides her. Priyanka pretended to sleep and Sapna also did not attempt to talk to her. This lasted for a few days.

Sapna would take full care of Priyanka but both would hardly talk to each other. Varun wondered if he ought to have insisted for Shikha to come. Finally, Priyanka broke the ice.

"Pass me my night cream," she asked Sapna. As Sapna got it for her, Priyanka held her hand and made her sit next to her.

"The pain gnaws at me. It is not just the physical pain but an emotional angst that is clutching me. I feel helpless and a prisoner of my thoughts,"she confided to Sapna, who remained quiet for a while. She then went to her suitcase and brought out something. Priyanka cried when she saw what it was. It was a photograph of her late chachu and chachi.

"The pain has never left me, didi. I have had nights like this for years. While acceptance came gradually, the pain stayed," Sapna said sombrely. "Why did you never reach out to us?" Priyanka said but then realized the futility of her own words. She recalled how they had isolated Sapna from their lives. "I am so sorry," she continued. "Both Shikha and I were unreceptive to you. We saw you not as a sister who needed us but as an intruder in our home. And yet, you carried on with courage, never uttering a word against us. Please forgive me, I realize now that love and care are the most vital aspects of any relationship. You were so young back then, but you handled everything in a very mature way. Even now, you are wiser than us."

Sapna stayed calm as Priyanka vented out her pent-up thoughts. She had already seen a change in her the other day when she had called up; now the present upheaval had made Priyanka more reflective. She had often overheard Sanjay and Mamta discuss her troubled situation and she could sense Priyanka's role in it but she could not have spoken anything. Now, she decided to guide her elder sister with all her sagaciousness.

"Didi, at times we question the situation in our lives. And at times, we think it is of our making but the truth is, life is all about change. It is all about moving on. No two days can be same and similarly no two persons can be alike. If we remember this, then automatically our expectations will reduce and not bring in anguish. I always missed my parents and thought what my life would have been like if they were around; and before the trauma of such thoughts could destroy me, I would force myself to think what if all of you were not around. Thus, I survived didi, feeling grateful for what I received and taking care to nurture it."

Priyanka was amazed at this little powerhouse of sanity. "My own Gautam Buddha," she exclaimed as she hugged her warmly and felt more at peace than she had in days.

❖

In the ensuing days, Priyanka healed more. Varun also came to terms with the episode and seeing Priyanka recover, was able to feel a sense of normalcy. He took extra care of her, and she often felt grateful for such a loving relationship. She was also extremely proud of Sapna and told it openly to her.

Sapna was delighted to find her elder sister becoming so fond of her. It was a bonus in her life and she knew that Shikha's attitude would show a change soon. She decided to go back and asked Varun to make the arrangements. Mummyji declared she was going to miss her a lot and along with her blessings, she made sure to give a handsome amount to her to buy something she liked. Priyanka too gave her a small gift she had ordered online. Once she left, they were back in their routine, leaving the unfortunate incident quite behind them.

Two months passed in a content space. The worst of the virus was getting over. The peak that had claimed many victims was finally gone and in the new lingo – the curve was flattening. The lockdown had been gradually lifted in a phased manner. Masks, hand hygiene and social-distancing were still imperative but at least, people could venture out. Fatigued of being indoors, people were resuming work and outings. As the trials of the vaccine progressed, life was inching back to normalcy. Varun kept extra occupied in his work and the bliss at home gave him new energy.

Spurred by the positive vibes, Varun felt exceptionally close to Priyanka and frequently found himself humming love songs. He often felt his true honeymoon was happening now. The Hong

Kong trip had been short and hectic, besides he hadn't really known Priyanka then. After that, the conflicts had rather driven him away from her. Now, the sun was shining and he wanted to express his love for Priyanka. He promised to himself to plan for a new trip as soon as the situation would permit.

His friend Chand called him up one evening. "Hey, buddy, I have some good news to share."

"Any good news is welcome in this scenario. Though I have guessed it, but want to listen from you. Out with it," Varun replied. He had never forgotten Chand's timely help during their crisis. Chand had been going steady but the epidemic had stalled his wedding. Now, he was all set for it.

"Yes, I am getting married to Fiona. You and Priyanka have to be there. The guest list is very restricted so count yourself lucky that you made it there," Chand joked. Varun laughed with him. It was such a welcome event. They had not stepped out in ages for any social function. It would be a good outing for them. He shared the news with Priyanka.

"Wow, I am so excited. It will be fun to dress up and go out. Let me arrange my outfit as the date is just a week away. Plus, I have to find a matching mask," she replied. Varun was amused at this latest fad going around – face mask as a fashion accessory had really caught up. He himself was satisfied with the plain and effective surgical masks but he knew Priyanka was fond of matching it with her outfits.

"You look so pretty," mummyji said as she saw the dressed-up Priyanka. Dressed in a royal blue sari with golden embroidery, Priyanka looked like a bride herself. Varun couldn't take his eyes off her and together they reached the venue where only around fifty guests were invited. It was a Christian wedding and Priyanka absorbed all the fine arrangements with wonderment.

As the couple exchanged their vows and resolved to be there for each other until death do them part, Priyanka felt lot of emotions stirring in her. The commitment expressed towards each other by the bride and the groom touched her deeply. She also recalled how certain she had been of everlasting happiness when she had gotten married. She sighed as she remembered all the unhappiness of past years. Golden days had been wasted in squabbles. She shook herself out of her thoughts and leaned towards Varun.

"I know what you are thinking, dear," he said softly. "But all that is behind us. I look forward to the rest of my journey with you." His thoughtful words cheered her up and she started enjoying the gala feast. She was impressed to know that Fiona had pursued an MBA and doing well in the corporate world. She suddenly wanted to do well in her career too and kept on thinking about it in the days that followed.

❖

"I want to enrol for an MBA programme," said Priyanka as they enjoyed a lazy Sunday brunch of aloo paranthas and raita. "That would be very nice and helpful for your career growth," Varun immediately spoke. Alka nodded and Jagat expressed his views too.

"Yes, I think higher qualifications would go a long way in giving a boost to your career profile. We will also say with pride that our daughter-in-law is an MBA degree holder." Priyanka felt happy to hear these encouraging words. She had thought about her career prospects and realized that her current work place had limited scope for growth. She wanted to rise to a senior management position and was ready to work hard for that. Unlike earlier times, she had shared her desire to study further with the family and got their support. Motivated, she took leave from her office and used the time to finish the admission formalities. She joined a correspondence course with specialization in HR. Shikha teased her when she shared it with her. "Oh my god, the study bug has bitten you, of all the people. I can't believe it's the same you."

Shikha herself was enrolling for Ph.D now as she wanted to be a professor ultimately. She had sensed the change in Priyanka though Priyanka refrained from talking much about it. She also had not shared how the miscarriage had shaken her. But today, Priyanka seemed in a talkative mood and so Shikha expressed what was in her heart.

"Didi, you seem happier nowadays. I have noticed that since some time. Besides, you also seem a different person than what you were. I understand you have undergone a lot but still, is there any particular reason?"

"Well, no, I am just glad that we could tide over the storm created by the deadly virus and mummyji and papaji are hale and hearty. I realized their blessings are a boon in our lives. And surprisingly, that realization manifested in a thousand ways which makes everyone feel I have changed. Maybe I am more flexible in my views now and I do not feel the need to react to every situation. That's about it."

"Wow, didi, so much *gyaan* and you say that's about it. Why, you are speaking like a spiritual guru – the one who has got enlightenment. But tell me, how you cope with so much work and all household chores now – you were never that type."

"These are small things if you keep looking at the bigger picture called life. Relationships have to be nurtured and a lot of effort does go in that, but in return, you get the beautiful gift of serenity, growth and love."

While Shikha was happy that constant friction was no longer there in her sister's life, she did give a piece of her mind to Priyanka. "All the wisdom is fine, didi, but compromising perpetually would sooner or later give rise to frustrations."

"But, I am not compromising. I am doing things for them because I feel like doing it. Moreover, relationships are about giving and taking, one sided approach doesn't work. I have learnt it the hard way. Once you accept people as your own, making efforts for them comes naturally, and it is reciprocated. Just see how much mummyji cares for me now. Papaji has become so motivating. Even when the miscarriage happened, they were like solid rocks of support," Priyanka explained patiently to Shikha.

"I have also been meaning to tell you that in this process, I realized how harsh we have been to Sapna over the years. Yet she does so much for all of us, without an iota of expectation. I have really learnt a lot from her as well. You must also start perceiving her from this view point and you will see a change in your equation with her. Rest of the relationships, you'll understand when you get married," she concluded.

She knew dad was now anxious for Shikha's marriage and she hoped they would soon find a good match for her. She made up her mind to visit them soon.

16

Inner Radiance

One day Varun came back from office and as usual, let himself in with his keys.

"Hello," he called out. "I'm home." No one answered. Perplexed, he went to his parents' room but no one was there. He walked towards his bedroom but that was empty. He heard sounds from the bathroom. The door opened and Priyanka came out, wiping her forehead, looking very drained.

"Are you okay? What happened?" Varun asked with concern and moved to hold her. Priyanka relaxed in his arms, and then whispered, "I think I am pregnant."

"What!" Varun exclaimed with wondrous joy. As the momentous impact sank in, he almost lifted Priyanka up. Priyanka told him to be cautious as she was still feeling giddy.

She sent him to get the test kit for confirmation and Varun rushed down to get it quickly. The test confirmed the good news and both felt ecstatic. Priyanka shared the news with mummyji when she returned from the walk.

"I am so delighted at this news. I will be a grandmother. Let us thank god whole-heartedly and get *prasad*," she gushed. She also sent Varun down to get some sweets and offered them in their small temple first. She broke the news to Jagat, who also felt happy at the thought of becoming a grandfather. While the earlier incident was in everyone's mind, it was pushed away resolutely. It was a blissful family that went to sleep that night.

In the days that followed, Priyanka further blossomed into a different person. Everyone told her to just take rest but forgetting her fears, she took care of the whole house enthusiastically, without any complaints. It was *her* house, after all. The doctor told her to be active and not think about the past. She too didn't want to look back and focussed on feeling energetic.

Cooking, cleaning, mopping, dusting nothing seemed to be too much. Everything in the house was spic-and-span. Everything at its correct place! The maid had still not been told to start coming, but that didn't seem to trouble her one bit. Mummyji and Varun helped her continuously and all chores were evenly divided with a shared sense of responsibility. She attended to her office work as well. The course was due to start soon and even her early morning nausea was subsiding.

Dad and ma had been ecstatic with the news too. In fact, Mamta made plans to visit her along with Shikha. Priyanka again felt gratitude for such loving relationships.

However, she soon developed back-ache and the doctor prescribed total bed rest for a while. She was immediately worked up about the household. Alka was very worried but her concern was more for Priyanka's health. She had a discussion with Varun.

"Look, in this state she should not do so many household chores. I feel much more energetic now and can surely do cleaning work apart from cooking."

"No, mummy, that's not feasible, I don't want you falling ill in any way again. I will take leave and manage somehow. Or we can start calling the maid and ensure she follows all necessary steps and keeps a distance." Varun spoke his thoughts aloud.

Priyanka overheard them and wondered how to find a solution. Soon, she would not be so agile and then would need help. But they all were really scared of calling the maid back. The virus was still lurking and till the time vaccination happened, they were not totally immune.

It was Jagat who provided the solution. "Let us put this house on rent and take a bigger house on rent. There are flats that come with a servant room attached. Then, we can have a live-in house help. This will ease out our problem and Priyanka will get support later on too. Also with the baby, we will, as it is, need more space in the house." Priyanka was touched by the concern showed by papaji.

Varun agreed with his father and together they launched an intense hunt for a bigger, spacious apartment. They soon found one in the suburbs but as the work-from-home culture was there to stay, commuting was not an immediate concern.

❖

Priyanka, Varun and family shifted to Kandivali in a roomy apartment that had three bedrooms and a small study. There was a servant room outside, which had been their prime requirement. They soon found a maid who was a widow and looking for a house as well. Radha bai as they came to call her, made life much easier for them with her efficiency and quiet demeanour.

Priyanka was able to get rest and she started to enjoy her free time. Mummyji introduced her to *Ramayana* and other such books and she tried to read through them to imbibe inspiring life lessons. Varun had started going to office and Priyanka knew sooner or later, her office would resume work as well. One day, she confided in mummyji. "I am going to find things tough. I would soon have to start going to office. Commuting will not be easy. Besides, I have my MBA classes to attend and do assignments for. My back is still delicate and I can't stress much," she poured out her troubled thoughts. Mummyji understood her but wondered where all this was leading.

"Beta, I understand you have too much on your plate. But you have to try to be stress free," she tried to calm her down.

Priyanka continued to feel bewildered. She later discussed her issues with Varun.

"I have come to the conclusion that I must discontinue my MBA, It will ease off my load and I can always do it later," she spoke to Varun.

Varun stroked her hair as he thought about it. "It's totally your decision. Just follow your heart. There is no compulsion of any sort," he soothed her. Priyanka snuggled unto him and was soon asleep.

Varun couldn't sleep and kept thinking about how to put Priyanka at ease. He also marvelled at the fact that how different the relationships were now. Priyanka had confided first to mummyji and then to him. Unknown to him, at that moment, Alka was sharing all the details with Jagat. And Jagat, as usual, guided them all with alacrity the next morning.

"Look Priyanka, I am aware that you are feeling disturbed. And none of us want you to feel this way. But my view is that instead of dropping your MBA, you should quit your job for the time being. This will give you ample time to cope with your studies and relax too."

"But papaji," Priyanka struggled to express that leaving the job would affect the finances of the house, more so now they had to pay rent too. Jagat understood her and again said, "Beta, you don't have to worry about anything. Between Varun and me, we will manage well. We can't put you to trouble of any kind because of a few thousand rupees. So relax and give notice in your office."

"I agree with papa, Varun also said. In fact it should have occurred to me but it didn't. This is a good way out. Later, once your MBA is complete, you can start again."

"And don't you worry about the baby, even when you do join office later on," Alka chipped in. "I am there for you in all possible ways. In fact, I can barely wait to hold my grandchild in my arms." Everybody laughed aloud and Priyanka thought about her financial independence but she knew that this was the only way to resolve her problem.

Priyanka mailed her resignation notice, the next day. She recalled her joy in getting the job and now she could feel a sense of ease in quitting it. Every feeling in life was ephemeral –that was the lesson she was learning. The month-long notice period was quickly over and soon, Priyanka found herself with lots of spare time. She delved into parenting books and shared her insights with mummyji, who would laugh all this new age drama away.

"When you have grandmothers around, you don't need books," she would say to Priyanka. She also missed ma. They had not met for nearly a year now. As the travel restrictions were lifted, Priyanka had been asking Mamta to visit her. She was pleasantly surprised one day.

❖

Shikha and ma visited her for a week. Sapna had stayed behind with dad. Shikha had a seminar to attend and later, she took leave to spend time with Priyanka. Ma was delighted to find her glowing. She was also impressed with the new house and Radha bai who made their stay comfortable. Shikha was amazed at how Priyanka had transformed. It was not just an external change in terms of cooking or doing household chores. There was an inner radiance that reflected on her face.

"I can't believe you are so domesticated. You were such a fireball earlier," she teased Priyanka.

Priyanka smiled and said, "Well, you only get burnt in fires."

Mamta indulged her by making and feeding her favourite dishes. "Don't take so much trouble, ma. And don't feed me so much. I am already looking like a potato," Priyanka protested. Mamta was amused at the comparison and reminded her how much she and Shikha loved the potato cooked in any form.

Mummyji enjoyed their bonding and asked Mamta to come at the time of delivery too. The delivery was not too far away now; Priyanka was already in her last trimester. Mamta was happy to see the pleasant environment that now prevailed in their home and she happily narrated all details to Sanjay on phone.

The day they were to leave, mausiji called up from Chandigarh. Alka was all praise about Priyanka to her and Mamta felt a sense of pride as she overheard the conversation. Priyanka felt a little sad as the duo left but then soon got occupied in her studies. Her exams were also coming up.

❖

One day, Varun's general manager called him over to his chamber. Varun was a little nervous, because he only interacted with the regional manager, who was his immediate superior. With the general manager it was only a 'good morning' or 'good evening' if he happened to meet him in the corridor. So he knocked on his door with trepidation.

"Come in," called the general manager from inside. Seeing Varun at the door, he added, "Good morning, Varun. Come in and shut the door, please."

Varun walked in and stayed standing, clasping and unclasping his hands nervously.

"Please sit down. I wanted to talk about your performance and your work, Varun."

Without my reporting head being present? This is against all protocol. It must be something really bad, thought Varun.

"I have been getting several reports of your performance from different departments and a few customers..."

There it comes, thought Varun, and braced himself for the impending bad news. The general manager paused and gave Varun a smile.

"And it is all good. In fact, excellent! You went beyond the call of duty when the virus was raging and never shied away from responsibility. You travelled even at that time and were meticulously involved in the vaccination programme."

Varun gave a huge sigh of relief. *So what has he called me for?* He wondered.

"Today, we have received the great news of the approvals for the vaccine coming in. So we have decided to spread cheer among our hard working staff too. We have decided to promote you. You will be a regional manager from today. Congratulations."

"Thank you, sir." Varun was obviously elated. "But what about my present regional manager? Where is he?"

"You know he belongs to Kolkata. He has decided to go back there. We are trying to find a position for him in the office there. East is a large region and extends from East UP to the northeast. We should be able to find something suitable for him."

"That is wonderful news, Sir. When do I start?"

"Right away. Go to HR first. They are waiting for you to give you a briefing. They will arrange for you to have sessions with other departments. From tomorrow, you will spend time with your regional manager and complete the knowledge transfer process. He is here for three days. After that you are on your own."

"Best of luck," he added, getting up and extending his hand for a handshake, indicating the meeting was over. "I have great expectations from you. I hope you will fulfil to them."

Varun shook hands with the general manager. "I will make sure I do. Thank you for placing your confidence in me," he said.

It was only when he came out of the room did the news actually sink in. Regional Manager! Wow! He wasn't due for this promotion for several years. He wanted to shout and express his delight. He couldn't do that in the office here. He took out his mobile and called Priyanka.

"Guess what? I have been promoted as regional manager!" he told her excitedly.

Priyanka, was overjoyed. "Congratulations. Fantastic!" she exclaimed. "Why don't you come home now? We'll celebrate right away."

"No, I can't do that. I have to go to HR for a briefing and then to other departments. I can't skip that."

"So can I come over and give you a big hug and a kiss between your meetings?"

"No, no, that won't do," laughed Varun, pleased by her reaction. "I will finish work and come home as soon as I can. Then we'll celebrate and you can do whatever you want. Meanwhile, you watch the TV, there is more good news coming up."

Varun disconnected the phone and counted his blessings again. He was in a happy zone and was feeling quite rapturous.

Priyanka switched on the TV to find that all the news channels were full of the vaccine for the deadly virus getting approval from the Indian Council for Medical Research. Finally, life would soon return to normalcy. She shared the positive developments with mummyji and papaji, who were extremely delighted to hear about them. "The baby is going to be the lucky one, Look at how he is already bringing so much good news," Alka said lovingly.

And so their first born had been named Shrey- the lucky one!

❖

Priyanka broke out of her reverie. Shrey and Abhiraj had fallen asleep. So had Varun. It was almost dawn but

Priyanka was wide awake. Visiting her past always made her introspective.

The past decade had seen professional growth for both Varun and herself. After his promotion, Varun had soared up, shouldering all responsibilities with ease. Unlike his colleagues, he did not jump from one company to another and that ensured a steady rise. Priyanka's MBA had also equipped her with a successful career. She had joined a fashion house soon after Shrey turned one and revelled there. Her natural sharpness, now coupled with a sense of empathy, made her an excellent HR resource.

She had again taken a break when Abhiraj was born but was poised for a promotion now. She looked graceful, her inner serenity and gratitude always reflecting on her face. They lived far more comfortably than they could have earlier imagined. She, along with Varun, were saving to buy their dream home soon. Varun had promised her a home full of all comforts- a home where they would spend their retired lives together and she looked forward to that. Personally, she still counted her blessings twice.

After Shrey, Abhiraj had brought further joy to them. Both kids were vivacious and a soothing balm to their grandparents. Mummyji and papaji, though quite frail now, remained the bedrock of their family.

Shikha and Sapna had also got married and were busy in their family lives. Their parents were still in Ambala but visited them often. Priyanka had no reason to complain whatsoever and she often wondered if she deserved all her good fortune. Varun told her she did. He was extremely proud of her and told her that often. Feeling grateful, Priyanka finally dozed off.

In the morning, the alarm went off and it was just another day, wherein she got up, supervised the maid, sent kids off to school, had breakfast with mummyji and papaji before driving off to work.

Epilogue

"Dadi, tell me a story," shouted the young Avyan.

For a five year old, he was chirpy and naughty. He shared a special bond with his grandma, who had perfected the art of storytelling.

"Which story you want to hear," asked Priyanka softly, adjusting her specs and ruffling Avyan's hair affectionately. Prashvita, the three year old younger grandchild also tried to climb on her lap and tried to mouth 'story'.

Shrey peeped in her room and smiled at the familiar scene. He was stepping out for a drive to meet his brother, in his aero car, with his wife Natasha. He and Abhiraj met for coffee every week and sometimes, Priyanka joined them. So he bade them all good night and left them for their story-telling ritual.

Avyan again pulled at Priyanka's kaftan. "Tell me beta, which story you want, shall we get the story book out?" she asked.

Despite living in a digital world, she still believed in the magic of storybooks.

"No, no, I want to hear from you, the story of the bad virus, which made all of you stay in the house," Avyan said. Priyanka wondered why he was so enamoured of this story. Though she could narrate it effortlessly, it revived too many memories, even after all these years.

But looking at the child's insistence, she tucked them both in bed and started telling the story. Soon the children were fast asleep.

Her mind wandered again. She felt a strong sense of déjà vu. Not so long ago, she was telling the same story to Shrey and Abhiraj. Time had flown. Twenty-five years, to be precise.

Shrey, currently a successful entrepreneur, was married to Natasha and had these two lovely kids. Abhiraj was working as an astro-physicist in the US and she was perpetually forcing him to get married. A lot had happened in the past years. She was sixty-five years old now, and the wrinkles were showing up, despite all her anti-wrinkle creams.

She still used them though, out of sheer habit. She sighed and getting out of the bed, went to the living room. The room automatically lit up to the dim lighting she preferred at this hour. Taxie, their robot, asked her if she would like her black coffee, which was what she had these days. She smiled at her new world. But her gaze was drawn to the wall. She thought of her loved ones and the life-like pictures came alive. She looked at the pictures of mummyji, papaji and dad- all had left her over the years. Her frail ma stayed mostly with Shikha now. Her eyes were glued to the last picture-Varun.

She still could not accept it. Just two years ago, she had lost the love of her life to a massive cardiac arrest. All the advanced technological equipments of the world could not save him and neither could all the scientific advancements tell her where he had gone. They had been bereft. Shikha and Sapna had stood by her and brought her back to a semblance of sanity. Her heart warmed up at the thought of her sisters. Both were in Mumbai now, with their families and close to her- just the way she wanted. They themselves had shifted to a penthouse in Worli after Varun's retirement, a few years ago.

They had invested together for their retirement abode. She finally had a house in her name but now without Varun, she frequently felt lonely. Shrey and Natasha took good care of her and she often thought that mummyji's blessings had held her in good stead. Her equation with Natasha was friendly and loving. Priyanka sometimes teasingly asked Natasha to call her mummyji but Natasha would stick to mom. Avyan and Prashvita were the cynosure of her eyes and a reprieve from her loneliness.

She thought how Avyan had termed the virus 'bad'. She thought of the lockdown time. No doubt, it had been a devastating experience to live that year– full of panic, anxiety, fear and worry.

But as she always told herself, it was the virus that had unlocked love for all of them and made them a happy family. It had not only brought about a remarkable shift in her perspective, but also made her the Priyanka, she was today.